New York

CYNTHIA EDEN

MW01515926

A VAMPIRE'S CHRISTMAS CAROL

This book is a work of fiction. Any similarities to real people, places, or events are not intentional and are purely the result of coincidence. The characters, places, and events in this story are fictional.

Published by Hocus Pocus Publishing, Inc.

Copy-editing by: J. R. T. Editing

CHAPTER ONE

He'd always wondered what it would be like to give in to the call of the darkness. To stop caring about what was right and wrong. As Ben Prescott stared into the terror-filled eyes of his prey, he smiled. "It's going to hurt," Ben warned.

The man within his grasp whimpered.

"But then, you've hurt plenty of people, haven't you, Miles? That's why I chose you." The snow fell lightly down on Ben as he held his prey pinned to the brick wall of the alley. "If anyone deserves some pain, I think it's you."

"Pl-please, buddy," Miles Gavin begged as he fought futilely to escape Ben's hold. "Just let me go, just let me—"

Ben bared his fangs.

Miles stopped begging then—and fighting. The terror in his gaze doubled as shock seemed to hold Miles still.

Yes, that was the usual reaction of Ben's prey.

Ben shook his head. "You thought that you were the monster people needed to fear." Miles had taken plenty of victims. Miles seemed to particularly enjoy hurting women. Women that he abused and humiliated before he finally ended their misery. "You were wrong." Ben drove his fangs into his prey's throat. The blood flowed over his tongue, hot and powerful. Miles still wasn't fighting him. As if a human's strength could have stopped Ben.

"Let him go, Ben." The voice was low, rasping, and far too close.

Ben lifted his head. His prey sank to the ground. Still alive, but only barely.

A siren screamed in the distance.

"The cops are coming," that rasping voice told him. "You need to get out of here before they find you."

"I'm not finished with him yet..." Miles still breathed, so Ben's work wasn't done.

"You truly want to kill him? Come on, death is too easy..."

Ben wouldn't know how easy death was. He'd only been dead for about two minutes before he'd risen again. "Who the fuck are you?" Ben snarled.

It was night, Ben's preferred hunting time, but his vision was perfect. He could see better than any cat in the darkness. That enhanced vision was a little perk of his undead condition.

The voice had come from the mouth of the alley, but shadows hid the speaker. The shadows were unnatural, though, a trick of magic, and he couldn't see through them.

"I'm your second chance," the voice told him. A man's voice. Vaguely familiar. "You should probably say thanks now, and, you can also wipe the blood from your chin."

Ben swiped the blood from his chin, and then he leapt toward those shadows. He wasn't afraid of magic. Ben wasn't afraid of anything or anyone.

When you were a vampire, you didn't have the luxury of fear.

You had the thirst for blood.

You had an endless span of nights stretching before you.

And you had power. So much power. Enough to push a sane man right over the edge.

His fingers closed around the speaker, and he shoved the man out of the alley. The shadows dissipated as the snow fell on them, and Ben found himself staring into a pair of bright blue eyes. Eyes that he knew.

The man before him was tall, just an inch or two under Ben's own six foot three height. The fellow's shoulders were broad, and his arms were covered with intricate tattoos. The tattoos also circled the man's neck. Swirling, dark tattoos that—if you looked at them closely—were moving.

I'd never forget those tats.

The guy in front of him wasn't actually a man at all. William Marley was a demon.

"Remember me, do you?"

Only in his nightmares. Ben dropped his hold on William. Demon blood burned like acid in a vampire's mouth. He had no plans to make that particular SOB into a meal. Behind him, Miles moaned in the alley.

"Forget him," William murmured. The sirens cried out again, louder this time. "The cops will handle the human. As much as you want to do it, you shouldn't kill him."

"Oh, yeah? Why not?" Ben's hands fisted. "Do you know what he's done? How he *enjoyed* hurting them?"

William rolled back his shoulders. "I'm not concerned with Miles Gavin. I'm here for you."

Ben's heart slammed into his chest. Despite the stories that circulated, vampires were actually still alive. Their hearts beat. They needed oxygen to breathe. Their "death" was just a transition as their bodies stopped being weak and human and became something far more powerful.

But...*When a demon says he's there for you, hell is coming.*

"Since you remember me, I'm sure you easily recall the first night we met," William continued. The tattoos around his neck seemed to darken even more.

Ben did remember that night. He'd been a newly turned vampire then. Wild with power. Broken by grief. He'd found William in a cemetery. The demon had been getting the hell beat out of him by four shifters. Because he'd felt like dancing a few rounds with death, Ben had joined the fight. Only one shifter had managed to escape alive that night, and as for William...

"I owe you for saving me," William said softly.

The sirens were too close. The cops would be there any moment. "Screw the debt," Ben said as he pushed past the demon. He'd have to finish Miles another time. "You don't owe me anything." He started walking through the snow. The small town of Desolate, North Dakota, wasn't his usual sort of hunting ground. He'd only gone to the little town in order to find Miles. In the last ten years, Ben had become very good at tracking his prey of choice.

Killers. Rapists. The men who deserved to be hunted—and to become Ben's victims.

He trudged through the snow. The demon didn't follow him, and Ben was glad to ditch the guy. The last thing he wanted to do was talk with William Marley. The fellow reminded him—too much—of what he'd lost. Because when Ben had gone to the cemetery, he hadn't joined the battle to save William.

I went into the fight because I wanted to die.

Only he hadn't. Instead of the shifters killing him, Ben had been the one to take them down. No matter who or what he fought, Ben always survived, and he was left to walk this damn earth endlessly.

The police cruisers flew past him. Ben hunched his shoulders and pulled his coat closer. The cold didn't bother him. His body healed from nearly any injury, so when his fingers got too cold, they just started to reheat a few moments later. He healed and he lived and he *hated* it.

Ben walked through the small town until he found the pickup truck that waited for him. He'd left the truck near the town's lone bar. He jumped inside the vehicle and was back at his little cabin within moments. The cabin was a dump, but he'd stayed in worse places. Far worse.

And to think...once, he'd lived in penthouses. The world had been at his feet.

Now he spent his time in darkness.

He slammed the cabin's door shut behind him. Ben marched toward the empty fireplace and—

Flames erupted in that fireplace, shooting out at him. Swearing, Ben leapt back as the heat lanced over him. The flames rose, licking near the cabin's sagging ceiling.

Then Ben saw the demon in the middle of those flames. *William.* Demons could control fire at will. The tricky SOBs could also teleport any place they wanted, in the blink of an eye.

Humans didn't know about demons. They didn't know about shifters and vampires—well, they didn't know unless they were prey. By that point, it was generally too late to matter. The paranormal beings kept to the shadows, and the humans passed their days in blind ignorance.

"I don't remember inviting you inside," Ben snapped when the flames finally started to die down. The jerk demon had singed his ceiling.

Vampires and fire didn't mix so well. Fire could kill a vamp, just as surely as a stake and beheading combo. A stake alone wouldn't do the trick, not permanently. To keep a vampire from rising, the vamp's head had to be removed.

Or the vamp's body had to be burned until only ashes remained.

William laughed. "Your kind needs the invitation to enter. Not mine." The flames vanished. William's tattoos swirled. "I'm here to repay a debt, and that's exactly what I'm going to do."

Ben ground his teeth together. "I never meant to save you. Does that cancel the debt?"

William's blue eyes glinted. "No."

Hell.

The demon's head cocked to the right. His hair was long and dark, hanging to his shoulders. "Do you know what tomorrow is, vampire?"

Sure he did. He might be a vamp, but he wasn't an idiot. As he'd slogged through the town of Desolate, Ben hadn't exactly missed the decorations that hung from every storefront. "Christmas." Just saying the word made pain wrench through him. He'd become a vampire ten years ago, right before Christmas. He'd lost *her*, right after the clock struck midnight on what the humans thought was such a happy day. Ben raked a hand through his hair. "I fucking hate Christmas."

William's lips twitched, then he waved his hand toward the bare cabin walls. "That would explain the lack of decorations in your, uh, charming abode here. You know, a tree, some garland—shit like that would really liven up this dump."

Ben's eyes narrowed to slits. "You're a demon."

"Talk about stating the obvious." William sighed. "I'm a demon, but I'm not evil." His lips definitely twisted into a smile this time. "*And I fucking love Christmas.* I mean, seriously—presents? Spiked eggnog? How does it get better?"

Ben's temples started to pound. "Get out of my house."

"I don't know that this place qualifies as a house."

The demon was a total dick.

William shook his head. "Besides, I can't just walk away from you. That's not how it works." His gaze dipped around the little cabin once more. "Maybe I'll decorate it for you. I'm sure *she* would appreciate some Christmas touches."

Right. The demon was a dick, *and* he was insane. "There aren't any women here. Just one psychotic demon and—"

"A vampire who is getting his *last* chance to change." The words held no humor. Only cold, hard promise. "The others downstairs, they wanted to mark you as evil already. To just put your name on the list and consider your fate sealed."

Ben stilled. *Downstairs?*

"The folks in charge upstairs have looked ahead, you see, and they know what you're going to do."

Cold air seemed to fill the room.

"But I don't think you've crossed the line yet," the demon said with another shake of his head. "And since I owe you, I agreed to do this little routine once more."

Routine? Ben felt so fucking lost.

William shrugged. "I've done it a few times in the past. Sometimes it works." Sadness crept over his face. "And, sometimes there is no saving the lost." His gaze raked over Ben. "The debt I owe you *will* be paid by midnight. One way or another."

"I don't care if your blood burns," Ben said, pushed too far. "I'm about to drain you."

The fire flared again, and in the next instant, William was right in front of Ben. The demon was *fast*. "You should be more grateful. You're immortal. One of the most powerful vampires I've ever come across. But you're going down a dark and dangerous path, a path you don't want to take."

Ben offered him a grim smile. "It's the only path for me." Blood and death and demons. Yeah, that all seemed right.

"Once you wanted more." William grabbed Ben's hand. The demon's touch burned, and smoke rose from Ben's skin. "You just need to remember that. Remember who you were before."

Ben twisted his wrist, but, even with his vamp strength, he couldn't break free from William's hold. "Let. Me. Go." Or he'd be ripping the demon's head off in the next five seconds.

"I'm the first visitor of the night."

The first?

"There will be three, and in the end, the choice will be yours." William glared at him. "But I'm telling you, asshole, *make the right choice*."

Ben flashed his fangs and went for the demon's throat. He braced himself for the acid burn to come. He'd drunk from a demon before, and he knew that taste would be a real bitch.

Before his fangs could slice into William, flames erupted around them. *Surrounded* them. And Ben knew he was about to die. His last thought...

Finally.

CHAPTER TWO

Ben smashed, face-first, into the snow. He leapt up and spat out the snow that filled his mouth. "What in the hell—"

"Not hell," William cheerfully told him. "Been there, done that plenty. This is New York. Your old town."

Ben whirled around. His gaze darted to the left. To the right. Sure enough, he recognized the buildings that shot so high up into the air. *New York*. He'd lived and breathed in this city for so long.

He'd also died there, temporarily, anyway.

His gaze focused on the entrance to Central Park. He'd been in there when his "death" happened. It had been so stupid to walk in the park that night. But he'd had plans. Such grand, hopeful plans.

His parents had loved that park. Before they'd died, he'd gone there with them so many times. The park had seemed to be the perfect place to start the future he craved.

But there'd been no future for him in that park. Only death.

"Let's just take a closer look," William murmured. He grabbed Ben again with his white-hot, burning hold, and in the next instant, they were inside Central Park. The snow was thick on the ground, and, in the distance, Ben could hear the sound of singing.

Christmas carols.

He'd heard those same songs ten years ago. Ten long years...

"Ah...let's see..." William's head turned to the right. "I figure you'll be here in five, four, three, two..."

A man walked out of the darkness. A man who wore a long, flowing coat. The fool didn't even have a cap on, and the snow left flecks of white in the fellow's black hair. The guy's shoulders were hunched against the cold and—

The man looked up. His green eyes darted around the park. Ben's breath caught as he stared at the guy.

That's me.

And just how was he staring at himself? What was William doing? How was this even possible? Ben grabbed William's shirt-front. *"What is happening?"*

William frowned down at Ben's grabbing hands. "Have a care. That's an expensive shirt."

What? The shirt had survived fire. Ben was pretty sure it would survive his grip. A growl broke from Ben's lips.

William sighed. "Magic makes it possible, okay? Some very powerful magic."

Ben's hands fell to his side.

"You're seeing a memory, my friend," William told him flatly. "So don't bother trying to call out to anyone. They can't see you. They can't hear you."

Seeing a memory...

"And, unfortunately—"

"We're not friends," Ben said, but the words held no heat. He was pretty much too stunned for heat.

"Unfortunately," William pressed on, "this isn't one of your better nights. This memory is gonna suck for you."

No, no, it wasn't a good night. Because even as Ben stared in shock, he saw a shadowy figure leap out from the trees. That figure hit his old self. *How fucking crazy is this? I'm watching the attack that ended my human life.*

Watching it and hating it.

The attack was fast and vicious, and blood sprayed on the white snow as the vampire sank his teeth into his prey's neck.

Ben lifted a hand to his throat. He remembered the feel of that bite. As if a thousand razor blades had just sliced into him.

As he kept watching, too stunned to speak, Ben realized that his old self was still trying to fight. Swinging out, punching. But a human was no match for a vampire.

And the guy that had attacked him this long ago night had been a very, very strong vampire. He looked at the vampire, noting the man's blond hair, so blond it was almost white, and the vamp's ashen complexion. The vampire fed on Ben for so long and then...

The vampire tore his mouth from Ben's throat. "Welcome to the darkness," the vampire hissed, and he cut open his own wrist with a quick swipe of his fangs.

"This is it," William said, his voice almost sad. "This is the moment it all changed for you."

The blond vampire shoved his wrist over Ben's mouth.

He'd only tasted a few drops of that blood, Ben remembered. Just a few—

The vampire laughed. Laughed and leapt away. The blond vamp raced back into the darkness, leaving a trail of blood drops in the snow behind him.

"He can't see you." William was studying the prone figure on the ground. "We're watching a memory, and the memory doesn't watch back. So go on..." His hand slammed into Ben's back. "Get a close-up look at what you were."

He didn't want a close-up look.

Ben could hear a faint, desperate, gasping cry. That had been *his* cry. He'd been choking to death on his own blood as he lay in the snow.

William shoved him again. "Don't be scared, vamp, it's not like you don't know what will happen next." His touch scorched Ben's flesh.

Dammit, Ben was tired of the demon's burning shoves! He turned around and drove his fist into the demon's face. *Take that, bastard.* William fell into the snow and Ben...he whirled back around and watched himself die.

The blond vampire had used his fangs to rip into and *across* Ben's neck. The wound was deep. Savage. Blood was all around his body. His eyes were open. Desperate.

So this is what I looked like when I died.

Chalk-white face, helpless stare. A mouth that struggled to speak, but with his throat ripped open, no words would be coming from him.

There was only...death.

And death did come. The gasping, choking sound ended with a wheeze. His eyes were still open, but staring sightlessly ahead. His chest didn't rise. The blood...it was a blanket around him. His final shroud.

Snow crunched beneath William's feet as the demon moved closer. "Now this only lasts a few minutes. The faster the rising, the more powerful the vampire."

Ben glanced over at William. The demon was swiping snow off his body.

"You came back damn fast, so that meant you'd be a powerhouse."

A powerhouse who'd never had the chance to cry out for help before his *change*.

But, sure enough, Ben saw the body in the snow stiffen. The green eyes changed, becoming golden in color, and the gaping wound in his neck...it closed.

The seconds ticked past in silence.

"You were lucky," William added, his voice low. "I knew some poor bastards who didn't rise until they'd already been buried. At least you didn't have to dig your way out of a grave."

Yes, he'd been...*lucky*.

Then the man on the ground—*me*—started to suck in deep, heaving gulps of air.

"You're back," William's wry voice told him.

Ben watched as his old self jumped to his feet. He ran shaking hands over his neck. Over his blood-soaked clothes.

"Back, but so different..."

Because the man standing there, with terror on his face...that guy had glowing, golden eyes...and two inch long fangs.

"I don't want to see anymore." Ben spun away from that memory or flashback or psychotic hallucination. Whatever the hell it was, he didn't want to watch it anymore. He locked his fingers around William's arm. "Get me out of here. *Now.*"

William lifted a brow. "It's because you know who'll be coming next."

"Get me out of here!"

"But if I did that, you'd miss the whole point of this walk down memory lane." William shook his head. "We're not done in your past yet."

"This is ridiculous! I don't want—"

"This is a lesson, and it's your last chance." Then William's eyes widened as he stared over Ben's shoulder. "Here she comes."

Ben almost bit him. *No, no, no.* Ben did not want to see this. Her. He didn't want to see *her.*

His heart pounded hard in his chest. *Please, no.* She needed to run away. Run—

"Ben!" A woman's voice called out. Worried. Scared. "Ben, where are you?"

"I don't want to see this," Ben growled.

"Ben!"

He found himself looking toward that desperate cry. *She* was there. She was bundled up in the coat he'd given her, with her long, blonde hair spilling down her back. As she called for him, her face reflected her fear. Such a beautiful face. Heart-shaped, with glass-sharp cheekbones and a small, straight nose. He would have been able to pick her out anywhere.

Gorgeous. Delicate. So very perfect with her dark brown eyes and her lush, red lips.

And, once...*so very mine.*

She spotted the man covered in blood. She ran toward him. Threw her arms around him. Held him tight. *"Oh, Ben! What happened? Where are you hurt? What can I do?"* Her hands flew frantically over him. Then... *"The blood..."*

I don't want to see this. The memory hurt too fucking much. It made him want to cut out his own heart. Right. Like he hadn't already tried that a time or ten.

Ben's eyes locked on William because he would not, could not, watch that scene any longer. "Simone should have left me in a bloody heap." *Simone Laurent.* The woman with the eyes that had seemed to see straight into his soul.

Until he'd stopped having a soul.

"Isn't that her ring that you had in your pocket?" William craned to see the couple over Ben's shoulder. "I mean, you were planning to marry the lovely Simone. That's why you came to the park, right? You asked her to meet you here so that you could propose to her."

He'd lost everything in that park. "Get me *out* of here."

"Um...you know, I'm not sure you're getting the point of this little activity." Now William's hand slammed down on Ben's chest, right over his heart. "Maybe you need a more *up-close* view of the past. Just watching isn't enough. Let's try experiencing it firsthand." William's tattoos started to swirl as the demon began to chant. Then he said, "I can only give you an hour, but I think it will be long enough. While you're there, it will be just like you're living things for the first time. You won't even remember me."

What. The. Fuck?

"So just enjoy your time with her. The end will be the same, no matter what you do. It's still a memory, only one you're living."

Ben could smell the scent of his own burning flesh. The snow fell harder, and then the fire raged once more, seeming to surge right up from William's hand.

Ben screamed as he was consumed. But it was *her* name that he screamed. Simone. The only woman he'd ever loved.

The woman he'd killed.

"Simone!"

***

Water slammed into his face. Ben blinked as steam rose around him. He shook his head and realized—

I'm in a shower.

Not just any shower, though. His hand flew out and yanked against the gleaming, gold faucet. He stumbled from the shower, his feet slipping a bit on the marble tile. This bathroom—it was in his New York penthouse.

He whirled around, his gaze flying to the left, to the right. *My place.*

"Ben, I've got a towel for you."

He stiffened. That was Simone's voice. He could smell her. That light, sweet scent of vanilla that had always clung to her.

Naked, dripping, he turned to face her. She stood in the doorway, a white towel held in her hands.

A dark wave of d éjà vu swept over him. He felt as if he'd somehow lived this exact scene before. With her. And...something very bad had happened. The knowledge was there, but...clouded. Foggy.

"Ben?" Simone gazed up at him with worry clear on her face.

He backed up a step. "You should...stay away from me." He wasn't even sure why he gave her that warning.

Simone shook her head. Instead of getting away from him, she said, "I want to help you." She crept forward until she stood right in front of him. Her right hand rose, and her soft palm settled against his chest. That one touch electrified him, and it sealed her fate.

"Please," she whispered. "I want to help you."

CHAPTER THREE

Lust clawed through him. The need, the red-hot desire, seemed to burn Ben from the inside. He grabbed Simone, yanked her flush against him. His mouth locked on hers. He'd always tried to be so careful with her in the past. Played the gentleman because she *mattered.*

He wasn't a gentleman any longer. Ben wasn't even sure what he was. He just knew he needed Simone naked, and he had to be *in* her.

He carried her back to his bedroom. He ignored the glittering New York skyline. She was the only thing he could see. Desire pounded through him. His cock was so swollen that he hurt and—

His teeth were extending. Stretching in his mouth.

Ben dropped Simone on the bed and stepped back, horrified.

"Ben?" Simone sat up on the bed and pushed back the blonde hair that had tumbled forward. "What's wrong?"

She was so gorgeous and sexy staring up at him. Looking at him with those wide, dark eyes.

I'm going to hurt her. He grabbed for the control that he'd always held so easily in the past.

Only that control was broken. Shattered. "You need to leave."

Simone sucked in a sharp breath. Pain flashed over her face. "I thought...you said you loved me."

He did love her, and that was why she needed to get the fuck away from him. "Something is different." He turned away from her so that she wouldn't see the fangs that were now fully extended.

Fangs. I've got fucking fangs now. When in the hell had that happened?

The bed squeaked behind him. "Nothing is different for me."

Her scent deepened. She'd risen from the bed. She was coming toward him. Ben squeezed his eyes shut.

"I love you," Simone told him. "No matter what, *I love you.*"

"Please." He'd never begged anyone before. "You should...go..." Because she was too much temptation for him.

Her fingers slid over his shoulder. He was still naked, and that one touch rocked all the way through him.

"I want to be with you," Simone said softly. "Always."

Those soft words tore away the last shreds of his control. Nothing could have stopped him in that moment.

Need erupted. A dark, consuming need that swept away the man he'd been. He whirled back toward her. They hit the bed together, and his hands flew out, ripping away her clothes.

Simone arched into his touch. She should have been shoving him away. She should have been horrified. Instead, she was caressing him. Making the need grow so much worse.

He licked her breast. She had full, round breasts with tight, pink nipples. He kissed them. Sucked them. Laved them with his tongue.

His heart raced in his ears, the rhythm fast and frantic. Wait...was that his heartbeat, or hers?

Ben pushed up on his arms and stared down at her. His gaze locked on her neck. On the pulse that pounded there. His breath heaved out.

Bite.

"Ben?" Her hands slid over his chest. "What's wrong?"

"I could...fucking...devour you."

She smiled at him. *Smiled.* When she should be running. But if she ran—

I'd follow.

Her legs shifted against him, parting more. His fingers slid into the haven there, pushing up into her sex. She was wet and tight, and she moaned when he thrust two fingers into her core. Her eyes held his. "I want you," she whispered. "All of you."

And there was no way he could hold back.

Ben thrust into her, driving deep in a plunge that left him balls-deep inside of her. She moaned and the sound maddened him even more. She was hot silk around his cock. So perfect. So...his.

He withdrew. Thrust deep. Again. Again.

Her fingers slid down his chest. He caught them. Pinned them to the bed. His mouth lowered over her neck. He licked her skin. Kissed her right over her racing pulse-point.

Raked her with his teeth.

Her sex gripped him tightly as she wrapped her legs around his hips. She arched up against him and that move pushed her neck against his mouth.

Her pulse throbbed beneath his lips.

His teeth raked her again.

He withdrew. Thrust. The bed creaked beneath him. He couldn't get inside of her deep enough. Couldn't thrust hard enough.

He wanted to claim her. Every single part of her. He wanted to *own* her.

"Ben!" Her sex contracted around him as she shuddered in release.

His own release pushed down on him, but he kept thrusting, not ready for that wave to hit him, not yet.

The smell of sex and sweet vanilla filled his nose. And her pulse...that racing pulse point, the fast rush of blood in her veins...it filled his mind.

His teeth sank into her throat. Blood—hot, rich, better than wine, better than *anything*— spilled onto his tongue. He kept thrusting and drinking from her. Taking and taking.

"Ben..." Her voice was a whisper now.

His climax hit him. The powerful surge shook his whole body, as wave after wave of release rushed through him. The pleasure was so intense that his muscles clenched. So intense he pulled his mouth from her throat and roared out her name.

But Simone didn't move.

And...as he blinked down at her, Ben saw the blood dripping from the two puncture wounds on her neck.

"B-baby?" Ben whispered. The burning lust was gone. The physical need slaked. And the desperate need for her blood? *Satisfied.*

He touched her cheek. Her skin was warm and soft beneath his rough fingers. She stirred, blinking, but her gaze seemed unfocused and too weak as she gazed up at him.

"What...what did you do?" Simone asked.

He was still in her body. Flush with release. And he'd taken her blood. Nearly taken her life.

His teeth had transformed once more. Returned to a normal size. A human size. He pulled from her body. So carefully now. Using the gentleness that he should have shown her before.

But he'd been a monster then.

That's what I am now. The blood. The fangs. The wounds from the attack that had healed so quickly. They were all the signs of what he'd become. Only Simone didn't see them for what they were. No, she didn't see *him* for what he was.

Ben left the bed. Simone reached out to him, but Ben shook his head. "I-I have to get a cloth for you. You're bleeding." She needed more than a cloth. The woman might need a transfusion. How much blood had he taken?

But her fingers curled around his hand. As he stood by the bed, she lifted his wrist toward her mouth. She pressed a kiss to his skin. "That was incredible," Simone told him, her voice husky.

What? He'd *attacked* her. Bit her.

He pulled his hand from her. "I hurt you." The blood was still dripping down her neck. And, as he stared at it, the dark hunger grew within him once more. He found himself leaning forward because he wanted to lick the blood away from her skin.

No.

He straightened. Backed away from her. Rushed into the bathroom and wet a cloth. He tried to suck in deep breaths, but they did nothing to calm him, and when Ben looked into the mirror—

My eyes are glowing. The gold gleamed with an unholy light. The man in that mirror, he didn't look like Ben. Not really. His cheeks were sharper. His mouth...crueler. And when he parted his lips, Ben saw the glint of his fangs.

Vampire. Those fanged freaks were only supposed to exist in movies. Books. But he was staring at one in the mirror. Gazing into a reflection that showed him a monster.

And here I thought vamps weren't supposed to have reflections.

"What's wrong?"

He spun and found Simone in the bathroom. Naked and perfect. He hurried to her. His hand was shaking when he wiped the blood away from her neck. *Taste it. Take her again.* The sly command came from deep within Ben.

He tossed the cloth away, but he could smell her blood. Blood and sex. A combination that seemed to be calling to a beast inside of him. "Leave, Simone," he managed to say.

She lifted her hand toward him. Her fingers were closed in a tight fist. "I-I found this a few minutes ago," she said, "when I was...I was moving your clothes."

Her hand turned over. Her fingers opened. A gleaming, diamond ring rested in her palm.

Pain stabbed into his chest. Into the heart that was hers. She'd possessed it from the moment he'd met her.

Simone's gaze was on his face. "This is why you wanted me to meet you in Central Park tonight."

His hand lifted. He took the ring from her palm.

"Why are you telling me to leave when you were planning to ask me to marry you?"

"Because everything has changed." In an instant. He shouldered past her. He had to get away from Simone and the scent of blood and sex. The lust rode him hard, and he was afraid, so afraid, that he'd lose control again.

He grabbed fresh clothes from his closet. Dressed as quickly as he could, then Ben hurried down to the lower level of the penthouse. He rushed by the Christmas tree. A huge, fourteen foot tree that he and Simone had painstakingly decorated.

He hadn't put up a tree since his parents died. He'd been cold and empty, just going through the motions of life.

Then he'd met her.

"Ben, wait!"

If he waited, they'd fuck again. And he'd drink from her once more. *No.* He wouldn't take her blood. She was already too pale. The woman might not survive another attack. And, worse, he might not be able to stop if he tasted her again. "I'm sorry." He shoved the ring into his pocket. "If you won't go, I will."

"It's Christmas!"

He glanced at the grandfather clock. Almost midnight. Just a few minutes away.

"Don't do this!" Her footsteps rushed toward him. "Whatever is happening, we can handle it. Together. We can—"

She touched him. A dark desire seemed to ignite at her touch. He twisted, grabbed her, and pinned her against the door. His mouth crashed down on hers. Hot and hard, and he thrust his tongue past her lips and he—

Blood.

The taste of blood filled his mouth. He must have bit her. Sliced her lip with his fangs.

Take more. Take everything. That was *his* demand, from a dangerous place inside of Ben.

For an instant, he imagined fucking her against the door. Driving deep into her and making her scream as he sank his fangs into her throat and took more of that delicious blood from her. He could take and take until—

Nothing was left.

He pulled away. Squeezed his eyes shut. "We're done." His voice was hoarse. Hollow. All emotion gone. There was no room for emotion.

Not when he was on the edge.

If I touch her again, I'll hurt her. Hurting her might not be all he did.

Ben was afraid he might kill her.

Simone put a hand to her mouth as she stumbled away from the door. He yanked that door open. Left her, before he broke.

"I love you." Her words followed him.

But he couldn't stop.

He ran toward the elevator. The whole damn area was filled with Christmas decorations. Bright red bows. Smiling angels. Sparkling lights. When the elevator doors opened, Christmas music spilled out to him.

The walls in the elevator were made of mirrors, and his twisted image glared back at him. Simone should have seen the monster when she looked at him. His golden eyes—his eyes should have been *green*. The fangs. The woman shouldn't have missed the fangs. He'd bit her, drank her blood, and she'd still whispered that she loved him.

He rubbed his chest. His heart hurt. *He* hurt because Ben feared he'd lost his life.

Central Park. His head jerked as the thought rushed through his mind. He just had to return to the park. Find the bastard who'd attacked him. Then he could make the guy undo whatever hell he'd wrought on Ben.

When the elevator's door opened, Ben lunged out into the lobby, then ran for the exit. He hurried out onto the busy New York street. Snow was falling, coming down harder with every moment that passed.

If I can find that bastard in Central Park, maybe things can go back to normal. Ben lurched forward.

Cars sped around him. Horns blasted.

"Ben!"

He heard Simone's cry, but Ben didn't stop. He raced across the street.

Brakes squealed behind him. A pain-filled scream ripped into the air. The cry chilled his blood.

There was a...thud. A sound that sickened Ben as he twisted around.

Time slowed then. He saw Simone—a black SUV had just hit her. The impact had thrown her into the air, and she bounced against the vehicle's windshield. The windshield cracked beneath her, and Simone rolled, sliding off the SUV's hood and falling to the ground.

Other drivers hit their brakes. There were collisions as the vehicles slipped in the snow and slammed into each other. The driver of the black SUV jumped out and ran toward Simone.

Ben could smell Simone's blood again. Only this time, the scent didn't call to the strange new beast within him. The scent terrified him.

Ben leapt across the street. He seemed to reach Simone in an instant. He grabbed the driver who was leaning over her. Ben hurtled the man back, then he bent over Simone.

Her eyes were closed.

Blood streamed from a gash on her head. And her neck...Simone's neck was at an unnatural angle. "No." He shook his head. His shaking fingers touched her shoulder. "Baby, *no!*"

Sirens screamed in the distance. He lifted his hand and put his fingers to her throat. Ben searched for her pulse.

Only there wasn't one.

Simone! This was their night. He'd planned it all so perfectly. A proposal in Central Park. Making love under the Christmas tree that she loved so much in his penthouse. He had presents for her. Dozens of presents that he'd wrapped and hidden upstairs.

Simone didn't have a family. She'd been alone, just like he was. They were going to start a new life together. They were never going to be alone again. *Always—together.* That had been his grand plan, just hours before.

Her pulse wasn't beating.

"Mister, I'm so sorry!" A man's voice. Coming closer. It was the fool he'd tossed away seconds before. "She ran right in front of me. I think she was chasing someone—"

She was chasing me.

And he hadn't even looked back at her.

Fear and pain twisted through Ben. But he bent, and carefully—*I should have used care before!*—he brushed his lips over hers. No breath whispered from her mouth. Simone didn't move at all.

The pain in his chest got worse. Burning at first, then...icing. Freezing him as the snow fell.

"Mister...mister, let's get her help!"

His beautiful Simone. She'd swept into his life just weeks before. Changed everything. She worked at the shelter on Forty-Ninth Street. She baked cookies for the people there. She—

Was gone.

He threw back his head and bellowed his fury as the pain engulfed him.

"Mister...?"

Ben spun around. He grabbed for the jerk's throat. "*You did this!*"

There were gasps around him.

"*Look at his eyes!*"

"*His teeth! Dear God, do you see his teeth? Those are fangs!*"

A crowd had gathered. They were screaming as they stared at him. As they turned and fled. Ben dropped the man in his hold. The fellow ran, yelling about monsters.

Ben fell to his knees beside Simone.

The snow had turned her hair white. *She's gone.* He felt her loss all the way to his soul. He reached for her. Scooped Simone into his arms. Held her close.

And wanted to die with her.

CHAPTER FOUR

"Well, that was painful..."

Ben's head jerked up. He wasn't in the middle of a New York street. Wasn't holding Simone's still body.

His hands were empty, and he was on his knees in a...cemetery?

"I didn't expect that little walk down memory lane to be such a pisser," William continued as he brushed snow off his shoulders. "I mean, I knew it was rough, but...fuck me, that got ugly. Especially with you being all desperate in the street." Then he paused and seemed to consider things. "Huh...I guess that explains why you wound up *here.*"

Ben surged to his feet. He grabbed the demon. "Stop playing with my mind!"

But William flashed him a smile. "That wasn't a mind game, friend. I told you. I was letting you relive that particular memory. Not everyone gets that—"

"I'm not your friend!"

"It was actually a gift. I gave you back—for an hour, anyway—the life you'd had." The lines around William's eyes appeared deeper. His face a little grayish. "And, just so you know, that sure sapped a lot of my own power. A *thank you* would be appreciated."

Ben's teeth snapped together. "You made me lose her again!"

"But you also got to taste her again. Got to feel her against you. What's pleasure without a little pain?"

"You're insane."

William seemed to absorb that. "Probably. See how you fare after you're sentenced to over two centuries in hell." His brows shot up. "But then, I'm trying to save you so that you *don't* have to become like me."

What?

"If you don't let go, I'll have to burn you again," William warned.

Then he just went right ahead and burned Ben's flesh before Ben had a chance to let him go. Swearing, Ben jumped back.

"*That* was for not saying thank you," William snapped. His eyes glinted. "Try a little courtesy next time. It *is* the holiday season."

Ben glared at him.

"This is the last part of my spiel, so don't worry, you'll be rid of me soon." William waved toward the cemetery in front of them. "This scene? It's another flash of your past. A movie-like version, playing right in front of you."

At least he wasn't having to experience this shit firsthand again. Ben felt like that last trip had ripped out his heart.

Because it had.

William stroked his chin as he seemed to consider the situation. "I figured we both needed to be reminded of why we're having all this quality time together tonight."

"I don't need to remember this place." He tried not to remember any of his past. It hurt too much.

But he didn't exactly have a choice. Over the gravestones and the frozen flowers, he saw the shadows. Five forms—fighting. The sound of grunts and the thud of flesh hitting flesh drifted in the air toward him.

"You're gonna die, demon. We're gonna slice every one of those tattoos right off you."

Ben found himself moving closer to the battle. Just as he had years before.

"This was the first time I saw shifters," he told William. "And the first time I saw a demon." He'd just thought he was jumping into a fight, until he'd seen the first man transform.

William was watching the fight before them. "You changed a lot of lives this night."

Then Ben saw his old self race from the darkness. He grabbed at the men attacking William. Sent them stumbling back.

One man hit a tombstone, then shot right back up—as claws burst from his fingertips.

"What the hell?" Yes, that had been his shocked reaction on that long ago night.

Because the guy didn't just stop with claws. The man's bones broke. Snapped. Reshaped. Fur burst from his skin. And in mere moments, a tiger stood in the man's place.

The other attackers started to shift, too.

They closed in and Ben...

In that memory, he just laughed.

Because I thought I was about to die. And I was happy. I was going to be with Simone. I had nothing to lose.

"They didn't expect your strength." This came from William as he watched the scene unfold. "You're a rare vampire. Stronger than even an alpha shifter."

And Ben did take down the shifters. With his teeth. With his hands. With a strength that he'd never imagined.

Until only one shifter remained. Not a tiger. A panther. The panther didn't attack. He lowered his head, showing submission, then he turned...and he fled.

"Why did you come to my aid?" William asked Ben as the images of the others faded away. The demon studied him a moment, then continued, "You didn't know me. I was a stranger, but you risked your life for me."

Ben smiled at him. He knew the demon would see his fangs. "I didn't fight for you. I fought because I was hoping they'd put me out of my misery."

William sucked in a sharp breath.

"That didn't happen. I'm still here." *And she's still gone.* The snow was falling again. How fucking perfect.

Ben turned and walked away from William. The demon had said this was their last little show. He was more than ready for William to end his magic routine. This night had been a mind-screw from the beginning.

"If death was all you wanted..." Now William's voice was deeper, seeming to echo with power. "Then maybe I can oblige you."

Ben tensed. He started to whirl back toward William, but the demon tackled him. William shoved Ben's face into the snow. The blade of a knife slid across Ben's throat.

"I could take your head, but that would be too easy," William's words grated in his ear. "And you don't get easy. Neither one of us gets that." The blade cut across Ben's throat, drawing blood but not severing his head. "Remember what you've seen...*and be prepared for what comes next.*"

Snarling, Ben twisted beneath the demon. He ignored the burn of the knife as he punched out at William—

***

Ben's fist drove into the wooden wall of his cabin. He knocked a hole right through that wall, and cold air blasted inside.

"William!" Ben bellowed.

But the demon didn't answer.

Ben yanked his hand back. He spun around. Searched the small cabin. There was no sign of the demon. Ben's eyes narrowed. Was this another game? Another mind-screw that the demon was using to jerk him around?

But...it *looked* like Ben was back in his cabin, the little place in Desolate, North Dakota. The fireplace was empty. No more giant flames leapt from its depths. The cabin was ice cold inside and growing more so with each moment that passed, thanks to the new window that his fist had just installed.

"Stay away from me!" Ben yelled as he glared at the fireplace. "Do you hear me, demon? No more visits! No more games! Keep your ass *away* from me." Or he'd finish what the shifters had started in that cemetery.

A soft rap sounded at his door.

Ben tensed. Had he *not* just told the demon to stay away?

The knock came again, more insistent this time.

"Go away!" Ben snarled.

But his visitor knocked once more.

He stalked forward, more than ready to beat a certain demon back to hell. He yanked open the door.

A demon didn't stand on his threshold. A ghost did.

Her blonde hair slid over her shoulders. Her dark, warm brown eyes met his. She smiled. "Hello, Ben."

Simone.

CHAPTER FIVE

Simone stared into Ben's stunned eyes. Her gaze swept over his face. A face that had haunted her for so long.

High forehead. Strong cheekbones. A long, hard blade of a nose. And that jaw—the wonderful square jaw that she had loved to kiss.

"You're dead," he gritted out the words as he stood, frozen, in the doorway.

Simone let her stare sweep down his body. His shoulders were so broad. His arms and chest were muscled and powerful. He towered over her own five-foot-four frame and—

"You're dead!"

His shout had her gaze snapping back up to his face.

Ben's eyes were wild. "Is this another one of the demon's games? Does he think it's fun to torment me with images of you?"

In that moment, her heart broke even more.

"I already see you in all my dreams," he whispered. "I think I'm tormented enough."

Even though she wanted to crumble, Simone pushed back her shoulders and stiffened her spine. She'd known this wasn't going to be easy. She just hadn't realized how much it would hurt to see him again. "You're dead, too," she heard herself blurt.

Then she winced. That was hardly the introduction she'd intended to use with him.

His dark brows shot down.

"I, um, I mean...you're undead." That was the deal with vampires. Not totally dead and far, far from mortal.

He grabbed her. Yanked her against him and *into* the cabin. Since he'd pulled her inside, she considered that an invitation to enter.

"Be real," he rasped against her mouth, and then he was kissing her. She'd missed his kiss so much. He'd always kissed her as if he were desperate for the feel of her mouth beneath his. As if he couldn't get enough of her.

Simone's fingers sank into the thickness of his hair. She stood up on her toes as she tried to get closer to him. He was so solid and strong against her. So real. So...hers.

He tensed. His head lifted. His eyes blazed down at her, glowing now with the power of the vampire. "You're dead."

"You keep saying that," she whispered. Simone licked her lips. She could still taste him. She wanted to taste him again.

"A dream? Is that what this is? Am I just dreaming about you again?"

She shook her head. "This is a visit," she told him, fighting to keep the emotion from her voice. She'd fought so hard for this time with him. "I'm the second one to come and see you tonight."

His brow furrowed.

Jeez, hadn't William explained things to him? "Your life—your soul—is on the line, Ben. Tonight is your last chance." His only chance. And she was so glad that she was with him. "Three visitors will come this night. One for the past. One for the present." She swallowed. "One for the future." She didn't want to think about the future. She'd already glimpsed what could come, and it terrified her.

"I'm crazy," Ben said flatly, but he didn't let her go. "I've lost the little sanity I had, and I'm imagining you now."

This was the part she dreaded. Simone exhaled slowly, and she let her own power slip out from her. Her shoulder blades tingled, then warmed as—

"You've got wings." He leapt back, moving a good five feet in less than a second. "Fucking wings!"

She knew her wings—long, white, rather fluffy, especially when she got nervous—were fully extended. "When we met before, there were some...things...you didn't know about me."

His jaw dropped in shock.

"I was in New York because I was looking for you. But I...I wasn't supposed to actually make contact with you." She sure hadn't intended to get physically involved with him, but Simone had broken all of the rules for Ben. "I was assigned to...help you. To guard you."

He shook his head.

"I *was* your guardian angel." Did he notice the emphasis she'd just put on "was" in that particular sentence?

Ben shook his head again as he walked toward her. His hand lifted and he reached out to carefully touch one wing. "It's real."

"The wings are real, and so am I." They didn't have much time. This one night was the only shot that Ben had been given. "I'm sorry that I couldn't stay with you." She'd wanted to be with him. More than anything. But—

She'd changed.

He was still staring at her wings with something close to wonder in his eyes. "Why didn't I see them before?"

Simone focused and slowly, inch by inch, her wings grew smaller. They kept shrinking until...*now you don't see them.* "You remember the scars on my shoulder blades?"

He'd seen them. Kissed them. Asked how she'd gotten them. She'd lied to him and said that she'd been in a car accident when she was twenty-two. Well, technically, that had only been a partial lie.

She'd died in that car accident. As had her parents. But...she'd become something more in death. "The scars hide the wings. When I'm in the mortal realm, the wings shrink in size and slide beneath the skin." Their small size made them little more than a ridge beneath her flesh. "When I go...home..." She didn't have a home any more. Hadn't, not in years. "When I go home, the wings return to their normal size." At least, that was what should've happened.

He spun her around. Stared at her back. She knew he'd be seeing the tears that were now in the back of her shirt. When her wings emerged, they sliced through her clothing. An angel's wings were soft, true, but they could also become razor sharp—depending on the angel's needs. When they were threatened, angels always used their wings for protection. It wasn't all about flight with those wings. It was about power.

Slowly, he turned her back around to face him. His expression looked so confused, so hurt, when he said, "I thought you died in front of me."

Tell him. "When I was twenty-two, I did die on a street like that one. My mom and dad—we'd just picked up our Christmas tree." They'd been so happy. Singing carols in voices that had been horribly off-tune. But that had been their tradition. *Get the tree. Sing the carols. Laugh all night during decoration time.* She cleared her throat. "A drunk driver hit my family before we could make it home. I survived for a little while, just long enough for an ambulance to get there, but I was dead before they could load me onto the stretcher."

She saw his eyes widen.

"I died, and I was given a choice. I could pass as others do, or I could try to...help. I chose option two and wound up with wings."

"You expect me to believe this?" Now anger snapped in his words as he stormed away from her and paced toward the small fireplace.

She didn't go after him. If she touched him...what would happen? Simone knew what she wanted to happen. *I want him, once more.* A memory to hold tightly in the darkness. But first, she had to make the guy see reason. "You're a vampire. If vamps can exist, if demons like

William roam the earth, then angels can be here, too. I mean, come on, you just saw my wings." What more proof did he need?

His laughter was bitter. "I *mourned* you. I blamed myself for your death." He whirled back to face her, and fear whispered through Simone when she saw the rage on his face. "When I lost you, I lost everything that mattered."

That had been the beginning for him. The beginning of the end. Her fingers twisted together. "If I could've come to you sooner, I would have." But the people upstairs hadn't known quite how to deal with her new condition. They'd thought they could help her. Heal her. Change her.

And all she'd wanted was to get back to Ben.

"Back in New York, I watched you for two years before I ever spoke to you," Simone admitted. She wanted to confess all to him, but she didn't know how much Ben could handle, not yet. "You'd buried your parents, and you were so consumed by your work." A millionaire with his star on the rise. He'd been vicious in business. Willing to do anything.

Willing to destroy.

"You were going down the wrong path. I just wanted..." She took a slow step toward him. "I wanted to help you. I tried to be your conscience, whispering when you were doing things that could come back to haunt you." Or to seriously bite him in the ass.

His bitter laugh came again. "*You* haunt me."

And he haunted her. "But I got too close," Simone told him softly. "It wasn't about guarding you. I wanted to...to be with you."

His head jerked up at those words. His gaze narrowed on her.

"I wasn't human, but you made me wish that I was." She would have traded her wings for him. Would have given her life, gladly, for him.

She'd loved him before he'd even spoken a single word to her. And when they *had* talked, when he'd kissed her, she'd been lost.

"You were jerking me around," he charged, voice rough. "From the beginning, you were trying to manipulate me."

His words hurt. Simone shook her head and took another step toward him. "Never, I promise. Ben, I'd *never* do anything to hurt you—"

He sprang at her. His fingers closed around her shoulders in a bruising grip. "*What do you think the last ten years did to me?*"

She didn't have an answer. No, she did, but Simone couldn't say the words to him. *Those years turned you into a monster.* Everyone else saw the monster when they looked at him. But she still saw the man he'd been.

The man who'd come into the shelter that day, looking so lost and out of place in his fancy coat. For so long, she'd been whispering to him that he needed to help others. *Help. Help.* She'd entreated for so long, trying to get him to hear her, and that day...he had.

He'd given his thousand dollar coat to the woman in the corner. Then Ben had rolled up his sleeves. Simone had taken human form that day because she'd been so happy to see him. So happy for the change that he'd made.

Ben had seen her. He'd come toward her. He'd helped her make lunch for the people in that shelter.

And he'd taken every piece of her heart.

"I was lost without you." His hold tightened even more. "I won't be lost again."

"Ben—"

He kissed her. Fury was in the kiss, so was desire. With the touch of his lips against hers, Simone knew the white-hot passion that had surged between them before was still as strong as ever.

Maybe she should have pulled away. Tried to get him to listen to her story. But...

I only have an hour. One precious hour with him.

Ben didn't realize the battle that was raging this night. She did. And if she could just show him the value he had. Show him that he was loved...

Her hands pressed to his chest. His heart raced beneath her palm. A fast, wild rhythm. She parted her lips even more for him. Kissed him with the desire that had remained within her for ten long years.

"I need you," he said, voice rumbling, as he began to kiss his way down her neck. She didn't tense when his fangs raked over her skin. There was nothing that his bite could do to her now.

She slid her hand under his shirt. His skin was warm, almost hot. In the movies, they said that vampires were cold. The movies were wrong.

So wrong.

He was like a furnace, and she loved that heat. It surrounded her. Banished the chill that had clung to her ever since she'd awakened in a morgue and realized that he was gone.

Her fingers slipped down, down, moving to the snap of his jeans.

"Simone?"

She undid the snap. Slid down the zipper. His cock sprang toward her. Fully erect. Thick. So hard. Simone lowered to her knees before him. He watched her with a gaze she couldn't read. Once, she'd been able to read him easily, but not anymore.

She could only hope her emotions were as hidden. She couldn't, *wouldn't* let him see the fear that curled within her. Passion would win this time. Desire would triumph.

Her fingers curled around his cock. She stroked him once, from root to tip. Again.

Then she put her mouth on him.

"Baby..." His fingers sank in her hair, but he didn't push her away. He urged her closer.

And she wanted to be close. She wanted to memorize his taste. Wanted to stroke and touch all of him. She kissed his heavy length. Loved the way his cock stiffened even more beneath her mouth. She loved—

In a flash, Simone was on her back. The old bed sagged beneath her, and her vampire stared down at her with his glowing, golden eyes.

"If I didn't know better," Ben said, his deep voice hard with desire and rage, "I'd think you missed me. But then, *angel,* you wouldn't have stayed away ten years if you really wanted me that much."

*If they kept me away, if they didn't give me a choice...*Simone swallowed back the words. They would only hurt him more. He didn't need to know what he'd done to her. "I want you more than anything," Simone told him, and her words were the truth. She wanted him enough to trade all that she had.

Enough to risk the dark that could come.

His hands flew down and a second later, her shirt went sailing across the room. Her bra followed it. Then his mouth was on her breast. He licked and he sucked and desire surged through her as Simone's hips arched toward him.

"Hurry," Simone whispered. "I need you now." Before time ran out for them.

He pulled down her jeans and took her underwear away with them. His own jeans were tossed to the floor. He positioned himself between her spread legs, and the broad head of his cock pushed into her.

Yes!

But he stilled. "Why?"

Simone shook her head. "Please, Ben, *now*."

"All these years...you should have come to me." His fingers curled around her hips. Lifted her up.

Then he plunged into her.

Simone moaned. Ten years. There had been no one else for her during that time. There never would be anyone else.

"I needed you. I wanted you." He withdrew. Thrust in even deeper. Had her eyes rolling back in her head as the pleasure lashed her. "You should have *come to me*."

His thrusts were rough. Frantic. His hands made sure that she met him, plunge for plunge as he lifted her hips up against him.

"I wanted to," she whispered, then Simone bit her lip. She couldn't say more.

"I'll be the one to bite." His mouth pressed to hers. "And I *will* bite."

His hand lifted from her hip. His warm, wicked fingers covered her sex. Found her clit. Stroked her as he thrust.

Her release was close. Her entire body tensed as his mouth slid to her throat.

"Do you still taste as good?" Ben demanded.

Speech wasn't really possible for her. The wild pants were pretty much all Simone could manage as her fingers fisted around the bed covers. He was driving so deep into her.

"I bet you do still taste as fucking good. Let's find out..."

His teeth sank into her throat even as he plunged into her again. His bite electrified Simone as pleasure erupted within her. His mouth...his cock...she cried out, lost, as her climax shook her straight to the core.

"That's right." Ben licked her neck. Kissed her. "You didn't come to me, but you can come *for* me." He lifted her legs up higher, opening her even wider to him as he thrust and thrust and—

He came on a hot burst of release inside of her. "*Simone.*"

Her eyes flew open. When had she closed them? And Simone saw her vampire staring down at her with a gaze gone blind with pleasure. She let go of the covers and held him as the pleasure continued to pound through them both.

Sex with Ben had always been phenomenal. Powerful enough to steal her breath. To make her shudder.

But it wasn't the sex that had bound her to him.

He pressed another kiss to her lips, but this time, the kiss was gentle. "I missed you," he confessed softly. The rage was gone from him.

It would come back. He still didn't realize what would happen that night.

But she did, and the pain already had her heart aching.

CHAPTER SIX

"It was my fault," Ben said as he stared down at her. He'd braced his hands on either side of her so that she didn't feel the weight of his body. "You were coming after me. You were hit by the SUV, because of me."

She shook her head, moving slightly against the pillow. "I didn't look when I ran after you." She should have looked. Angels could take the form of humans if they wished. She'd taken her old human body because she wanted Ben to be able to see her. To touch her.

But that body was vulnerable. When angels were flesh and blood, they could be hurt. They could be killed.

They could be...changed.

Angels were supposed to stay out of the sight of human beings. She'd been taking a huge risk just by assuming her human form so many times around Ben. "The choice was mine," she told him.

Most days, angels stayed in their astral forms. No one saw them that way. And angels, when they were in that astral form, they could fly right through cities. Right through buildings.

She'd been so used to the invulnerability of the astral form, that she'd forgotten how very fragile a physical body could be.

Until an SUV had hit her.

One instant, she'd been surrounded by a swirling world of white snow, and in the next moment, she'd only known darkness.

Later, she'd found out the darkness had been due to the body bag that she'd been put inside. The emergency personnel had zipped her up in that bag and tossed her into cold storage.

"Where have you been?" he demanded as his gaze searched hers. "All these years, where were you?"

She put her hands on his shoulders and pushed him back.

Ben's jaw locked, but he withdrew from her body. A long, slow glide that had her tensing. And, when he was gone, she missed the hard feel of his flesh within her. How many times had she longed for him? How many times had she called out for him in the middle of the night?

He positioned his body next to hers. Simone started to rise from the bed, but his hand flew out, and his arm settled over her stomach. "You're not leaving me again."

Yes, she was. Sooner than he realized.

Her gaze darted around the small cabin. "Why don't you have a Christmas tree?" She'd always loved Christmas trees. Their delicious pine scent. The way their lights twinkled. The homemade ornaments perched all over the limbs of the trees.

Perfect.

Her mom and dad had made sure she added new ornaments to their tree each year. When they'd...when they'd had their accident, a Christmas tree had been strapped to the top of their car. They'd just cut that tree at a local farm. They'd been so happy.

That happiness had ended with the scream of metal. Her parents had died instantly. Simone hadn't passed so easily. Her car door had cut into her side, slicing so deeply. Firemen had painstakingly worked to free her from the vehicle. They'd kept telling Simone that she was going to be all right.

She'd known they were lying.

"You convinced me to put up that tree in New York," Ben recalled as he pulled her closer. "You said the tree would make everything better."

Simone swallowed as she tried to push the painful memories from her mind. "Your penthouse was so...cold." Professionally decorated with everything in exactly the right place. *Too perfect.* Too sterile. "I thought the tree would give the place—"

"Warmth?" Ben's voice was flat. "Life?"

She gave a slow nod.

"No, baby, you did that. You brought the life. Without you, there wasn't anything left to celebrate." He ran his tongue over his fangs. "Especially when I became *this*."

"The fangs don't make you a monster."

His eyes narrowed.

"You should put up a tree," she whispered. "It will remind you of the way things were. When your parents were alive. When you were younger. Happier. When you believed that—"

"A fat, old guy in a red suit was going to make my world better?"

Her lips pressed together. Simone shook her head. "No, when you believed that there was more than just darkness in this world."

His hold slackened, and she slid from his grip. Simone found her clothes and dressed as quickly as she could. He watched her from the bed. Big, muscled, sexy...and dangerous. So very dangerous to her.

He didn't know what she was risking for him. Simone planned for him to never find out. "I'm your second visitor."

One dark brow hitched up.

"That means I show you the present."

"The only present I care about...it involves you coming back into this bed with me." He sat up, his jaw locking. "Once wasn't enough. A million fucking times with you won't be enough."

Her gaze fell to the floor. "We can't. Not now." The minutes were ticking past too quickly. Her shoulders squared. "Time is running out. Get dressed. We have to go."

He rose slowly. Had he missed the whole "time is running out" part? He dressed, never taking his eyes from her, then Ben stalked toward Simone. She exhaled on a relieved breath. "I move fast," she told him. Simone figured he needed the warning. Her wings spread behind her. "So just hold on to me. You can even close your eyes, if you want. When you open them, we'll be at our first stop."

"Screw that," he said as his fingers curled around her and he pulled her against him. "I want you to stay right—"

Her wings flapped. She locked her hands on him and shot into the air, nearly ramming into the roof of the cabin. Her hold jerked Ben up with her.

"Shit," Ben muttered. *"Shit."*

Simone almost smiled. Then she flew them right through the closest window and out into the night.

***

Ben's feet slammed into the ground and he nearly fell to his knees as his stomach finally left his throat and returned to its normal position. "What was that?"

Simone pushed back her long, blonde hair and grinned at him. "Angel speed." Her dark eyes seemed to shine.

He never wanted to experience angel speed again.

"It's how we can get to so many places in moments." She snapped her fingers together. "Just like that."

No, he thought it was more like the speed of light. Ben heaved out a breath as he straightened. The last thing he wanted was to look weak in front of Simone.

Simone. Her sweet, vanilla scent filled his nose. He could still taste her on his lips. She was real. Not some desperate dream. And he'd had plenty of desperate dreams about her over the years.

She wouldn't tell him where she'd been. But he would find out. It was only a matter of time. He'd find out all of her secrets, and then Ben would never let her go again.

Her wings were gone now as she approached the cell—an actual prison cell. She'd flown through an open window in the prison. They shouldn't have fit through that window, but she'd worked some kind of magic and—*bam*—they'd gotten inside. Ben didn't know why Simone had brought him to that dim prison but—

"I'm innocent!" A man yelled. Ben saw the guy's bloody fists curl around the prison bars. "You've got to believe me! I didn't hurt anyone!"

Ben took a few fast steps forward. He knew that voice.

"Don't worry," Simone said softly. "He can't see us or hear us."

The *he* in question—the man behind the prison bars—was Miles Gavin. Ben's lips peeled away from his fangs as a snarl built in his throat.

"It's an angel trick," Simone added. Her fingers slid over Ben's arm, as if she were trying to soothe him. "Angels usually move on the astral plane, and that's why humans don't see us."

The astral plane? That bit of info actually succeeded in temporarily pulling his gaze away from Miles.

Simone licked her lips. "I was granted...special permission so that my magic would cover you, too. We're in the astral plane right now—that's how we managed to fit through the window. Space and time distort here."

Well, at least that was one mystery solved. Or semi-solved. He still didn't understand half of the shit that was happening.

"Humans can't see us," Simone continued. "They can never see angels in this plane." She gave a faint shrug of her shoulders. "That's why you didn't see me all those times in New York. Before we met at that shelter, I'd been watching you for quite a while. You just never realized it."

Apparently, he'd missed one hell of a lot.

"*Let me out!*" Miles yelled.

Ben narrowed his eyes as he focused on the human. That man should already be dead. Instead, Miles looked far too *alive*. His blond hair hung over his forehead. A bandage had been applied to his neck. Red stained his cheeks as Miles shouted, "You've got the wrong guy! Please, *please!* It wasn't me!"

"Bullshit," Ben growled. "He's a murdering SOB. I should've ripped out his throat when I had the chance."

"Like you did to the others?" No emotion was in Simone's voice when she asked this question.

His muscles locked. "I'm a vampire. I have to feed in order to survive." It was kind of his thing. Ben figured an angel should know that.

Miles was still begging. Hell, it even looked like the man was crying. *Did your victims cry, too? Did they beg?* Ben knew they had.

"You have to feed, but you don't have to kill. That's a choice you make." Simone took a step away from him.

Ben advanced toward that cell. He was nearly right in front of Miles now, and the man showed no sign of being aware of his presence at all. Ben even waved his hand in front of the guy's face. *No response.* He glanced back at Simone.

"You can take from your prey and still leave them alive." Simone shifted a bit to the right when a guard entered the area.

"Leave them alive? And what? Let them turn out like me?"

Simone shook her head. "A vampire is only made—*usually*—if a human is drained of blood and then ingests some of the vampire's blood. There has to be an exchange." Her head tilted to the right as she studied him. "But after ten years, you're well aware of how vampires are made. So don't try to tell me that you kill them because—"

"I kill them because they deserve to die."

The guard unlocked the cell.

"They've killed," Ben said flatly. "Tortured. It's not like I'm hurting innocents." Were there any innocents any longer? Sometimes, he wasn't so sure. "I'm taking out the trash." He was doing a fucking public service. Simone should be thanking him instead of lecturing him.

"*You're free to go, sir,*" the guard told Miles.

Miles sucked in a deep gulp of air.

"No." Ben's hands fisted. "He killed five women. Strangled them. He—"

"The last attack victim survived," Simone said, cutting through his words. "But you knew that, of course, because she's the one who cemented your belief in his guilt. You looked into her memories, and you saw her attacker."

Angels weren't the only ones with special powers. She could fly and enter some damn astral plane. Vamps, on the other hand...vamps could compel humans. He'd learned that he could gain entrance into an individual's mind just by using a mild compulsion. Ben could use his power to see the person's memories.

When he hunted, he used those memories to guide him. He saw what survivors had witnessed. "I always punish the guilty." Because he was dead certain of that guilt. "Jasmine Duncan saw *him*."

The guard was leading Miles out of the cell. Ben hurried to follow the two men. *This was a mistake.* A huge, fucking mistake. Miles Gavin would just go out and kill again. He needed to be in the ground. He needed—

"Daddy!"

A little, red-haired boy ran toward Miles. The child threw his arms around Miles's legs and held tight.

And...a few feet away, another tall, blond man slouched in a chair. His wrists were cuffed in front of him. That man looked up at the boy's cry. *His face...the man had the same face as Miles.*

"Miles has a twin brother," Simone said as her arm brushed against Ben's. "Your victim didn't know that. Since she didn't know it, neither did you."

Miles sank to his knees and buried his face in his son's neck.

A twin?

Simone cleared her throat. "His brother stole his name. They shared the same face, so the deception was easy. Alex—that's his brother—he used Miles's money, he used his connections, and he took as much as he could from his brother."

Miles was holding tightly to the little boy.

"But there are some things you just can't take away," Simone murmured.

Ben looked over at her.

Her gaze held his. "Tonight was important for you. This kill—taking Miles Gavin's life would have changed you."

His hands were shaking. *I was wrong?*

"You're not meant to be judge, jury, and executioner." Simone's hands curled around his shoulders as she turned Ben to fully face her. "And you're not supposed to just be a monster hiding in the dark."

"So what am I supposed to be?" His voice was little more than a growl. He didn't know how to be anything other than a monster any longer.

"More," Simone whispered. "I need you to be more. For me. For yourself." He saw her wings began to rise from her back.

Oh, shit. "Wait—"

It was too late. His stomach hit his throat once more as they took off.

CHAPTER SEVEN

"Where in the hell are we now?" Ben asked as he jerked away from her.

"This is a long way from hell," Simone replied. "Trust me on that one."

He was shaken, she could see it. She'd hoped for that exact reaction when she took him to the little jail in Desolate.

Ben had almost killed an innocent man. If William hadn't stopped him, Miles Gavin would have died in that alley.

Instead, Miles would be spending the night with his son.

And she and Ben had returned to the alley in question. The spot that had started everything on Christmas Eve. "This is where you almost killed him," she said as she pointed to the dirty brick wall just a few feet away.

His eyes widened. "*You* sent the demon, didn't you?"

Yes, she had. She'd paid a heavy price for the night's work. "I wanted to save you." Okay, so maybe she'd never completely stopped watching over him. Maybe she couldn't. Love didn't stop, no matter how much time passed. "You were so intent on killing tonight that you missed a few things here…"

He growled at her.

"Don't bite the messenger," she told him, aware that her voice held more than a little bite of its own. "Because you need to hear this message." *While there was still time.* She exhaled slowly. "Maybe you should have gone a little deeper into the alley." She led the way as they advanced into the darkness of the alley. A dumpster waited in the far back, near the rear entrance to a restaurant.

She heard the rustle. Such a faint sound. Easily overlooked. *As overlooked as the person who'd made the sound.*

Ben grabbed her arm and pushed her behind him. Simone smiled. He was protecting her. It was sweet, really. The big, bad vampire—trying to shield her. She'd been right about Ben. He wasn't a lost cause, not yet.

"You're so busy punishing the world," she told him, her heart aching, "that you forget you can save it." *Help.* When she'd first been assigned duty as Ben's angel, she'd whispered that message into his ear so many times.

The rustle came again. She looked up and saw a hand curve over the edge of the dumpster. A second hand joined it as a young boy—around seventeen—pulled his body up and out of that garbage-filled bin. He was wearing old, mismatched clothes, and when he hit the ground, she saw that his too-big shoes were lined with holes.

"He saw you, by the way," Simone added. "When you nearly killed Miles, he was watching."

Ben's gaze was on the boy.

"That's Cale. He pretty much lives in this alley, but after seeing you, he's getting ready to rush off. He's afraid the cops will come back and find him here."

The boy's stare darted nervously around the alley.

"Or he's afraid that *you'll* come find him." Simone was pretty sure that particular fear consumed the boy's mind.

The boy ran past them. Simone could feel the heat of his body, just for a moment, then he was gone.

Ben stared after him.

"Cale hid when he heard you come into the alley. He jumped into the dumpster..." Simone wrinkled her nose. That dumpster was *foul*. "He stayed there until the cops were gone. You scared him so much that he was afraid to move...until now."

Slowly, Ben's stare came back to her. Though it hurt Simone, she had to tell him the rest. She took a deep breath and said, "You've become the monster in the shadows that others fear."

"I...didn't know he was here."

"But you should have known. You have vampire senses, Ben. They're far more enhanced than a human's. You should've heard him. Smelled him. *Something*. But you were just so focused on your kill that you missed what was right in front of you." And now the boy's life would be changed forever. Simone was so desperate to make Ben understand what was happening. One life could impact so many others.

For better.

For...worse.

One life could do so much good, or so much terrible evil.

The air around her seemed to grow colder. "We don't have much time left." She offered Ben her hand.

He didn't take it. "Can't I just walk?"

"Ben—"

"This little show and tell routine is interesting and all, but I'd rather not fly angel anymore if that's all the same to you."

She grabbed his hand.

"Shit," Ben muttered.

***

They touched down on an old, snow-covered road. Trees surrounded each side of the road. The leaves had long since vanished from those trees, and the gray tree trunks and limbs were frozen in the winter silence.

Simone pointed to the left. "This way will take you out of Desolate." She looked to the right. "And that path will just take you back to your cabin." Her gaze returned to his. Her dark gaze gleamed with emotion. "You have to choose the direction you take, Ben. It's all on you."

He stared into her eyes. There were deep golden flecks in her eyes. How had he missed those before?

"I don't want you to return to that cabin." She shook her head, and her hair slipped over her shoulders. "I don't want you closing yourself off from what *could* be in this world."

No snow was falling. Ben glanced up and saw that the sky above glinted with a thousand stars.

Simone's fingers caught his. "I don't want you to return to hunting and killing in alleys. You deserve more than just the darkness."

But that was all he knew. He hadn't known light since she left him. "He welcomed me to the darkness. That bastard who changed me. He turned me into...*this*."

"Most vampires do go dark. They can't resist the call of the blood. They...they lose themselves in the dark hunger that burns within them. The hunger for blood. For power."

Great news.

"I don't want that to be you. It doesn't *have* to be you." Her fingers tightened around his. "That's what this night is about. You're getting a second chance. You can see the world differently. *You* can be different tonight."

He didn't feel different. His tongue slid over his fangs. "I want your blood again."

Her breath caught.

"I can hear your heart pounding," Ben rasped. Because he did hear it. Calling to him. Tempting him. "I want to put my mouth on your throat, and I want to damn well devour you."

She should have backed away from him. Simone didn't. She inched closer. "Then why aren't you? Why aren't you biting me right now?"

"Because I don't want to hurt you." Not ever. His hand turned so that he was the one holding her. "If you stay with me, *I* can change." Hell, did that sound like begging?

"I-I can't stay..."

No. Fear clawed him from the inside. "You came back to me. You want me—dammit, I proved how much we both need each other back at that cabin."

"I've always wanted you," she said as her gaze held his. "Vampire or man, I want you."

"Then stay." He would make her stay. "You want me to be some kind of better vamp? Some fucking good guy? Then you stay with me, and I'll change."

"It's not that easy."

Bull. "It's as easy as we want it to be."

She looked away from him. Gazed into the darkness.

A strange awareness rose over his skin. He almost felt as if...as if Simone were staring *at* someone. But when he followed her gaze and peered into the darkness, Ben couldn't see anyone.

He wrapped his arms around her shoulders and pulled her closer to him.

"My hour is almost up." Her voice sounded so sad.

An hour? "Screw that. *Stay.* We can have forever."

"Ben..."

"I'll get you a Christmas tree." Those stupid words just burst from him. But he would. If the tree made her happy, he'd get one. He'd get her a thousand Christmas trees, and he'd string lights on every single one. "We can decorate the tree like we did before. *Everything* can be like it was before. You'll be with me, and I'll be—"

"I love you."

Ben's throat seemed to close up on him.

"I do." She smiled, and the sight twisted his heart. "I wasn't out of your life because my feelings changed. I was away because my feelings stayed the same."

That made zero sense to him.

"I love you," Simone whispered, "and I would do anything for you."

The snow started to fall again.

"You have worth to me." Simone gazed up at him with eyes that swam with tears.

He hated the sight of her tears. They broke him.

Her hand stroked his cheek. "You always will have worth to me, and for you, I'd even go into the darkness."

She rose onto her toes. Simone pressed her lips to his. He kissed her back. Desperate, greedy. Ben had never thought he'd get to hold her again. To have her in his arms once more was better than heaven, it was—

She vanished.

The snow fell harder, and Simone, she was just—gone.

"Simone?" He spun around in the snow. There were no sign of her footprints. Had she flown away? Moved at that angel speed of hers? He looked up, gazing frantically into the sky that no longer shone with stars. Snow fell down onto him. *"Simone!"*

But she didn't answer him. The cold crept into his bones. Rage bled through his pores. She had left...again? After such a short time? She'd come back, she'd screwed with his head, and she'd just flown away?

"No, angel," he vowed as he glared up at that dark sky. "You don't escape." Even if he had to fight his way up to heaven, he wasn't letting her go.

Simone had made a fatal mistake. She'd come back. She'd reminded him of everything that he'd lost on that New York street. He wouldn't lose her again.

I can't.

He also wasn't going to just stand there on that long, snow-filled road all night. He glanced to the left once more. Then to the right.

Just as he took one step, a growl rose in the darkness. Ben tensed even as his fangs automatically lengthened in his mouth. The fang extension was a vamp's fight-and-kill instinct, a natural reaction to danger.

A dark form emerged from the falling snow. Black, sleek, the animal came toward Ben with its head positioned low to the ground. But as the beast drew closer, that head lifted to reveal a mouth packed with long, sharp teeth.

That's not a damn dog. The beast leaned back on its hind legs as it prepared to launch toward Ben.

It's a panther. A black panther on a snow-filled night. A black panther who was hurtling toward him in a blur of speed. Ben lifted his hands, more than ready to fight the beast but—

But he wasn't staring at a beast any longer.

Mid-attack, the panther shifted. Its body stretched. The fur vanished and skin appeared. Bones popped and snapped and Ben soon found himself staring at a man.

The man's bright green eyes assessed him. "Hi, asshole," the guy said, his voice rumbling and sounding like a growl. "Remember me?"

Ben's gaze locked on the stranger's face. He studied that face and let his brows rise. *The panther from the cemetery.* "The last time I saw a panther shifter, the cat ran away from me."

The man smiled and waved his hand. The snow stopped falling. "I wasn't running from you. I was so happy you'd killed those bastards...I was starting *my* life. I was running toward my future, not from you."

Ben didn't relax his guard. Not for a moment. "I'm supposed to believe that crap? You and your shifter buddies were a pack." At least, he'd thought they were. They'd sure all attacked together. "You were fighting with them."

"It's not easy to kill an alpha shifter. Even if the prick is crazy as all hell." The man smiled. He had thick, dark hair and eerily bright green eyes. Ben had never seen eyes shine quite the way this shifter's did.

The fellow was also stark naked.

"You freed me from him," the shifter said. "So now, I owe you."

"Great," Ben snapped. Cause that was what he wanted. A cat saying he was grateful. "How about you put on some clothes and we'll call it even?"

The man waved his hand again, and clothes just—appeared. Jeans. A t-shirt. A t-shirt? In the winter?

"I don't get cold," he said. "Shifters tend to always be warm."

Wonderful for them. Ben shouldered past the guy.

"Ah, at least you're going in the right direction..."

The cat was following him. No, not following him. The cat shifter was right *beside* Ben now. The guy moved fast.

"I'm Jamison," the fellow said.

Ben whirled toward him. "Fuck off, *Jamison.*"

Jamison's green eyes narrowed. "I'm your last visitor for the night."

This was so screwed. "I don't want you." Ben grabbed the shifter by the t-shirt. "I want Simone back. Bring *her* back." She was the only visitor he cared about.

"Ah, enjoyed that little meet-and-greet, did you?" Humor flashed in Jamison's eyes. "But that angel is smokin', so I don't blame you a single bit for wanting to tap that ass."

Ben slammed his head into the shifter's nose. There was a savagely satisfying crunch of sound. Blood spurted. The shifter howled.

"Don't fucking talk about her," Ben snarled at him. "She's the woman I'm going to—"

"What? Marry?" Jamison pressed a hand to his bleeding nose. Then, not even pausing for a second, he snapped the broken nose back into place. "Sorry, man, but I don't see that in your future."

"Oh, you don't?" It took every bit of his self-control not to grab the guy and re-break his nose just for the hell of it. "Then what do you see?"

Jamison flashed a broad smile. One that showed way too many sharp teeth. "I thought you'd never ask." His hand slapped down on Ben's shoulder. "The future...that's what I'm all about tonight. Your future and that sweet-ass angel's future."

Ben's back teeth ground together.

Jamison pushed him forward. They started plodding through the thick snow. "She wasn't just *your* angel," Jamison told him as if confiding a big secret. "It's not like a one angel per person deal. They watch over a lot of folks at the same time."

Ben hadn't known that. Mostly because he didn't know anything about angels.

"I was her charge, too." Jamison stopped and stared straight ahead. "I used to think death would be my way out. The alpha was so freaking twisted. He cut on us just as much as he did his prey." Jamison's hand rubbed over his chest. "But then, maybe we *were* his prey." His hand dropped.

Ben's head tilted as he considered the shifter. Jamison's nose wasn't bleeding anymore. It wasn't even swollen.

"We heal fast," Jamison said, obviously reading the question on his face. "Almost as fast as vampires do. That's why I didn't scar, no matter how many times the alpha took the skin right from my body."

Fuck.

"The past can be hell, and the future..." Jamison exhaled on a rough sigh. "Sometimes, it can be a nightmare, too."

"I'm supposed to believe that you're about to show me the future?"

"I'm going to show you the future that *could* be," Jamison corrected carefully. "The real future is what you make it...or haven't you realized the point of this shit-forsaken night yet?"

Ben blinked.

"And it's not like I'm doing it on my own. We've got a special magic working for you. Courtesy of our angel girl." Jamison's gaze hardened. "For the record, I don't think you're worth what she's done, even if you did save my hide ten years ago."

What she's done... "What do you mean?" Ben demanded.

"I mean I'd let you rot." Jamison stalked forward. "If I had been given the choice between—"

"What has she done?" Ben caught the shifter's shoulder and whirled Jamison around.

And he heard a scream. A loud, desperate scream.

"There it is," Jamison drawled. "Right on time." He gazed at Ben. "Do you even react when you hear screams anymore? Or do you just not care?"

Ben threw him back and ran toward that sound. As he raced ahead, Ben realized that he could smell blood in the air. The scent was too tempting for a vampire. Ben rushed through the trees. He shoved the branches out of his way and he found—

Blood in the snow.

A boy, broken on the ground.

Ben stumbled to a stop. He knew that boy. It was the kid that Simone had shown him in the alley. Cale. The boy's torn, old shoes had fallen off his feet. They lay several feet away in the snow.

"Told you," Jamison announced as he slowly approached. He seemed to be taking his time. "The future can be a nightmare."

Ben swallowed and managed to ask, "Is this...is this what will really happen in the boy's future?"

"It's the future planned now, what *can* happen." Jamison's voice held sadness as he added, "He tried to run, but he wasn't fast enough."

Ben leaned over the boy. The kid's eyes stared sightlessly ahead. Two deep puncture wounds lined the boy's throat. The kid had screamed—and now Ben knew why the scream had been cut off so abruptly. A vampire had fed on the boy, and when the vamp finished his meal, he'd backed away.

You let him scream, didn't you?

Then the vamp had broken the boy's neck.

"He won't rise, so you don't have to worry about that," Jamison told him, voice cold and hard. "He's just going to get buried by the snow out here. It will be days before anyone finds the body."

Ben's gaze snapped toward the shifter.

"The snow plow will eventually come through." Jamison shrugged. "That's the way it is for some people. They die, and no one even notices."

Ben was noticing. The poor kid. Broken in the snow. He turned his head and looked back down at the boy. Just a teen. In someone else's cast-off clothes. No socks on his feet.

"If he'd stayed in the alley, he would have survived the night," Jamison noted. "I thought you might like to know that bit..."

Ben's shoulders tensed.

"The restaurant over there had a broken back window. Cale lived in that alley because he could sneak in the restaurant on cold nights. He could fill his belly and stay warm. But the boy was too afraid you might come back, so he ran tonight."

"I *wasn't* the vampire who did this."

"No, you weren't. There's another vamp in town, and you didn't even notice him. Seems like that happens with you a lot. The whole not-noticing-routine."

"This future sucks." Ben's hands were hard fists. The kid's eyes were so blank. Ben swallowed and asked, "What was his full name?" Simone had just called him Cale.

"Why? It's not like knowing will change anything." The shifter's hand pushed into Ben's back. "There's more to see. We don't have all night to stare at the dead."

Ben knocked his hand aside. "We're not just leaving him in the snow."

"Sure we are." That hand came right back to his shoulder.

Ben shoved it off again. "No, we're not." Ben looked down at the ground. "He's—"

Gone.

"We're looking at the future, vamp. He's not dead. Not yet." Jamison propelled him forward once more. "Let's see what else is waiting for you."

Ben didn't want to go anywhere. "Unless it involves Simone, I don't want to see the future that's coming."

Jamison stopped shoving him. "This night isn't about her."

"Yeah, well, guess what? I'm changing the rules. From now on...*it's about her.*" Because she was alive somewhere in this world. Maybe in heaven. *But she was alive.* "I don't go anywhere, I don't see anything, unless it's about her."

Jamison tilted his head back and stared up at the sky.

"You told me that I wasn't worth what she'd done for me," Ben nearly shouted at the guy. "I want to know what she did. I want to know what happens to her." *I have to know if she comes back to me.*

Jamison's head lowered. His gaze found Ben's. "Maybe I can show you her future...and yours. Both mixed together. That won't break the rules too much."

If their futures were mixed, then that had to mean she came back to him. Hope flooded through Ben. "Good. Do it, just—"

Snow swirled around them. The snowflakes were moving so fast that they almost looked like wings—an angel's wings.

The twisting, gnarled trees vanished in that blur of white.

"Remember," Jamison growled, "you asked for this."

Ben heard screams. Voices rising and falling in desperation. So many voices.

So much pain. So much fear.

What did they all fear?

Is it me? Did they fear him? In the future, what would he do?

But then the snow vanished once more, and Ben saw...*Simone.*

CHAPTER EIGHT

"Simone!" Ben cried out her name.

"Aw, man, come on." Jamison shook his head in disgust. "You know it doesn't work like that. This is your third freakin' time tonight with this crap. Get the drill down, okay? No one can hear you or see you in these visions. That's just how it goes."

Simone was walking in front of Ben. They were...in Desolate? Yes, the shifter had transported them back to the heart of the little town. Ben glanced around and recognized the town's lone bar. The bar waited just a few feet away.

He hurried to keep pace with Simone. She might not be able to see or hear him, but he had no intention of losing sight of her.

The bar's door opened. A man wearing a heavy coat staggered out. His eyes locked on Simone. "Well, hello, there, sweet—"

She grabbed him and rammed the man against the bar's outer wall. Then she sank her fangs into the man's neck.

"*Surprise,*" Jamison muttered.

Ben could only shake his head. *This isn't right.* "No, she's an angel!"

"Not in this future, she's not. Actually...she hasn't been a full angel in about ten years."

Ben's eyes were on Simone. The man wasn't fighting her. He couldn't. She'd just—she'd ripped his throat open.

Simone?

She let the man fall when she was done with him. Then she wiped her mouth, stopping long enough to lick the blood from her fingers.

And she headed into the bar.

Screams came moments later. Ben lurched forward when the cries erupted.

Jamison blocked his path. "You know what she's doing in there. Wasn't that—" He jerked his thumb toward the dead body. "Wasn't that enough of a future glimpse for you?"

Ben's gut twisted. "Simone isn't like this."

"You mean, she *wasn't*."

The screams quieted.

"I told you." Jamison nodded and flashed that toothy grin of his. One that held an evil edge. "She gave up a lot for you."

Simone appeared in the doorway again. Her blonde hair gleamed in the bar's light, and that light also clearly showed the blood that soaked her shirt.

"There's a price for magic." Jamison turned his head and watched as Simone walked away. The woman was even whistling. "Especially for the kind of mojo she wanted used on you tonight."

Ben peered into the bar's window. Three bodies were sprawled across the wooden floor inside that place. "This isn't her." He grabbed Jamison by his t-shirt once again. "This is some trick you're using to mess with my mind. Now show me her, the *real* Simone. Show me her future."

Jamison's hands came up, and four-inch long claws had sprung from his fingertips. "Move 'em," he ordered Ben, "or lose those hands."

Ben didn't move them. "Don't make me kill you, shifter."

"You mean...the way you killed Simone?"

That hit went straight to Ben's heart.

And so did Jamison's claws. Because they sank deep into Ben's chest. "Warned you..." Jamison ground out.

Ben pushed Jamison back as his blood dripped onto the sidewalk. "Bastard, you said you'd cut off my *hands.*"

"So I went for your heart instead. Maybe I was trying to see if you *had* one. I mean, use your freaking head. What do you *think* happened to the woman after you took all her blood ten years ago? You took her blood, and then you turned her."

No. Ben's gaze flew around the area, but he didn't see Simone. *I can't lose her!* "I didn't give her my blood." His frantic stare returned to Jamison.

"Uh, yeah, you did. It wasn't a lot, I'll grant you that much. The stories say it was just a drop or two, but that was enough to seal the deal, and enough to turn Simone into the first vampire-angel that the world has ever seen." Jamison smirked. "Come on, it's not like she was involved with any other vamp. Your blood did this to her."

And Ben remembered a kiss. A last, desperate kiss in his penthouse. His lips had crushed against

Simone's, and, for just a second, he'd tasted blood. "No," he whispered.

"Um, *yes*," Jamison tossed right back. "And let me tell you, a lot of powerful folks were sure shocked by that change. Angels aren't *supposed* to become vampires. Vampires are evil and dark, and they only exist to kill."

Ben flashed fang at him.

"My point exactly." Jamison flashed his own fangs, then said, "Angels are supposed to be good. They're the protectors. To see one changed like Simone, it shook up the people in charge. They kept her in lockdown until they could see what she'd become *and* what she'd do."

Ben brushed past the guy. Simone was close. She *had* to still be close by.

Another scream broke the night.

Ben ran toward that desperate sound. *Simone!* He just had to get close to her once more and then—

He rounded a corner.

And staggered to a stop.

This time, Simone's prey was a woman. Blood dripped down the woman's throat as Simone laughed.

"No!" Ben yelled. "This isn't you, baby! Stop!" She was the one who helped people. In the future, there was no way that Simone could become like *this*.

"Three freaking times," Jamison's voice was disgusted as he headed to Ben's side, "and you still act like folks in these visions can hear you. I *told* you, they can't. She can't."

Simone's hands rose. They curled around the woman's neck.

"Don't," Ben whispered.

Simone jerked her hands to the right. The snap of the woman's neck was too loud in the quiet of the narrow alley.

"Take a close look. What's *missing* from this picture?" Jamison asked, his words sharp. "I mean, other than the whole soul that Simone used to have?"

Ben's eyes burned. "She looks the same to me."

"You are such a fucking liar. That woman looks like a monster. Check the fangs, dude. Look at all of the blood that *covers* her."

Ben did, but in his mind, he still saw her as the woman he'd met in New York. The woman who had laughed so sweetly. When they'd bought that Christmas tree together, her eyes had lit up. She'd stared at him with so much love in her gaze.

After they'd decorated the tree, she'd kissed him. Promised him forever.

"Her wings are gone." Jamison's voice was flat. "But I guess you never really saw those anyway, did you? How can you miss what you didn't see?"

Simone started to whistle again as she walked into the night.

"Where is she going?" Ben asked.

"To kill again. That's pretty much all she does these days. But tonight...tonight will be different for her."

Ben had to swallow the lump in his throat before he could speak. "Why did she lose her wings?"

"That's the price for powerful magic. To save your sorry ass, she had to give them up. She traded her wings for your chance at redemption. Her wings...your soul."

Snow began to fall around them. Only...

Ben lifted his hand. *It wasn't snow.* Instead of catching an icy snowflake, he was touching a soft, silken feather. *An angel's wings.* His hand fisted around that feather. "*No.*"

"How else do you think you were able to see the past? And the future? An angel's wings are so powerful—they're the source of an angel's magic. Those wings can do anything. Even give a jerk like you a second chance."

The feathers swirled around them. Ben knew the feathers were taking him to Simone once more. Only it was a Simone he didn't know. He'd lied when he told Jamison that she looked the same. She didn't. She looked like a shell of the woman she'd been. All of the vibrancy, the *life*—it was just gone from her face and her eyes.

The feathers slowly drifted to the ground. Ben glanced around and saw that they were in a cemetery again. Simone was strolling through the graves. She paused for just a moment near what appeared to be a freshly dug grave.

"Fuck," Ben muttered because he knew how this part of the tale went. "Is that *my* grave?"

Before Jamison could answer, four shadowy figures sprang from behind the tombs in that cemetery. *Another cemetery attack...just like with William...*

Only Ben wasn't in this image. He didn't rush to Simone's rescue.

Simone spun toward her attackers, baring her fangs.

"Hunters." Jamison's voice was clipped. "Not all humans are clueless. Especially when you kill as boldly as she's been doing."

The men were armed. With—cross bows?

"Simone!" Ben lunged between her and the men just as one guy fired a wooden stake from his cross bow. The stake flew right through Ben's body, like he wasn't even there. *Fuck, I'm not.*

Then Ben heard a gasp behind him.

He spun around. Simone was still standing, but the stake had driven into her chest.

"She's hit!" Ben heard one of the men yell. "Close in! Take her head!"

Simone's fingers curled around the stake. She tried to pull it out of her body.

"Must've missed her heart," another man shouted. "I'll get her this time."

Simone's fangs flashed.

And another stake sank into her chest. She fell back and dropped to the ground.

Ben dove to his knees next to her. "Baby?"

She was choking. Trying to speak. Coughing up blood. But, even though she wasn't supposed to see him—*Jamison had been fucking clear on that*—her head turned. Her tear-filled eyes seemed to find Ben.

"L-love..." Simone whispered.

"I'll take her head," a man called out.

Simone's lips curled as her eyes sagged closed.

And a machete sliced toward her throat.

"*No!*" Ben bellowed.

But his angel was gone. Her blood spilled onto the snow, spreading beneath her like wings. The wings she didn't have any longer.

His breath heaved out, his lungs burned, and agony twisted Ben's body. *Not Simone. Not Simone. Not Simone.*

"Let's dump her body with the other vamp's. She sure seemed crazy enough about him. The bloodsuckers can be together in death."

One man grabbed Simone's feet. Another her—her head. Ben swallowed bile as he watched a dark-haired male drag Simone's body toward a freshly dug grave.

"You'll want to look close for this part," Jamison advised him.

Ben forced himself to move near the grave. He felt as if the wood had pierced his own heart. *This can't happen. Not to her.*

Jamison pushed him toward the grave. "I know...the flesh is all gone so it's probably hard to recognize yourself..."

Fuck. Ben craned his head and looked into that grave. He saw...bones. A skull. *His* skull?

The humans threw Simone's body in the grave. Her body and her head.

His eyes squeezed shut.

Why don't you have a Christmas tree? Her voice whispered through his mind. She'd loved those damn trees so much.

And...*she loved me.*

She'd been so giving. So open. *I want to help you.*

She'd looked him in the eyes. *I love you.*

She had. An angel, loving the monster he'd become.

Ben opened his eyes and saw that the men had started shoveling dirt onto her body.

"See?" Jamison asked as he slapped a hand on Ben's shoulder. "You're together forever."

Ben's heart stopped beating. "I'm really the skeleton in that grave?"

"Um, yes, you are. Simone didn't wind up saving you, but you...you sure introduced her to the darkness."

Welcome to the darkness.

"Simone couldn't handle the darker urges of her vampire side. Not once her wings were gone."

The men kept shoveling dirt onto Simone.

"Christmas Day." Jamison sighed. "She lost the last of her wings then. They were her gift to you, because she knew..." Jamison walked around the grave. "She knew that you'd wind up here. See, after you killed Miles—"

"I *didn't* kill him!" William had stopped him before he'd taken the human's life.

Jamison smiled. "Are you sure about that?"

Ben sucked in a sharp breath.

"After you killed Miles, you lost your hold on sanity. When it came to your prey, you didn't care about guilt or innocence. You gave in to the darkness. You drank from anyone, *everyone,* leaving shells behind. You became the true monster that everyone fears, and you had to be put down."

Simone's blonde hair was covered by dirt.

"And without you..." Jamison's voice roughened. "I think she was ready to die, too."

She'd smiled at him, in that last moment. Or had she smiled *because* it was her last moment?

Jamison pushed a hand through his hair. "Some people aren't made for the darkness."

Ben glared at Jamison. "This *isn't* happening to Simone."

The shifter's face hardened. "Then you'd better change your future, vamp. Because if you go dark, so does she."

Ben leapt toward the shifter. He grabbed Jamison's shoulders. "Take me to her! Not this twisted future. I want the real Simone, *now!*"

The wind began to howl.

The humans vanished. The cemetery vanished.

"It doesn't work like that." Jamison's voice was quiet, almost sympathetic.

Ben didn't want his sympathy. He wanted Simone. "Screw how it works. You know where she is. Take me to her."

"Earn...her..." Jamison broke from Ben's hold and dropped to the ground. The shifter's bones began to snap. "Save her...earn her..." Fur spread along his arms and legs.

"Do *not* turn panther on me!" Ben reached out for him, but the panther's claws sliced along his arm. "I need Simone!"

The panther opened his mouth and roared.

The snow fell again. No, not snow—*feathers*. Feathers from an angel's wings. She was losing more wings for him even then. Trying to teach him some kind of lesson? Trying to save his life?

But she was losing her own life in the process.

Ben tilted back his head and stared up at the sky. "I want her! Give her back to me, and I'll do anything!"

The howling of the wind grew louder.

"I can—I can change!" Ben yelled as loudly as he could. "Just...*don't let her die!* Don't let her wind up like—" *Me.* "Please, save her," he whispered. "*Please.*"

And everything went dark.

Welcome to the darkness.

CHAPTER NINE

The alley reeked of garbage and death.

"Pl-please, buddy," Miles Gavin begged. "Just let me go, just let me—"

Ben's fangs flew at his throat.

Then he stopped as understanding hit him—hard. *What the fuck? I'm back here?*

Ben shook his head as Miles trembled in his grasp. This was...this was the moment when the demon had appeared. Ben glanced toward the mouth of the alley, expecting to see William Marley's form.

But the demon wasn't there.

"I-I've got a son." Miles spoke quickly, feverishly, as he cried out, "He's only seven, and I'm all he's got. His mother's dead. Please, mister, *please!*"

Ben freed the man. "Go to the police. Tell them that your brother has been killing women."

"Wh-what?"

Sirens screamed in the distance. At least the cops were right on time. *Where's William?* "Screw that plan. You don't have to find the cops because they're coming to you. Stay here and wait for them. Tell them you didn't kill the women. Your brother did."

"A-Alex?"

"Your brother is a fucking psycho, so don't let him near your boy ever, got it?"

Miles pressed back against the dirty wall. Fear twisted his face as he stared at Ben.

The wail of the sirens was even louder.

"Forget you saw me," Ben ordered.

Miles lifted a trembling hand to this throat. Blood dripped down his collar. "What are you?"

"A monster." But he *would* be something different. For her.

Ben spun away from the human and raced into the night.

***

Ben burst into his cabin, dragging the Christmas tree with him. It had been the last tree on the lot, and Ben knew it looked like a piece of shit, but it was better than nothing.

Be here, be here. "Simone!" He'd spared Miles. Did that mean she would come to him?

His gaze darted around the cabin.

The place was dark. Cold. Empty.

She could come, though. I just...I have to get everything ready for her. He hauled the tree inside. Set it up. Ben set it up three times because the damn thing kept falling over. He lit the fire. And realized...

I don't have any ornaments. Not even a string of lights. And he also didn't have a present for Simone.

Wait...yes, I do! His gaze shot to the small chest in the corner. He hurried toward the chest. Opened it. Saw the little black box nestled inside.

He *did* have a present. One that he'd held onto for years. Ben shoved the box into his pocket. "Simone! I'm going to be different! I'm going to be what you need!" His bellow just seemed to drift back to him.

He paced toward the tree. "William? Jamison?"

No answer.

It wasn't midnight yet. A quick check of the nearby clock confirmed that. It wasn't Christmas. He still had time. Jamison had said...Simone didn't completely lose her wings until Christmas.

There was still time.

Ben hurried back to the door. He yanked it open and stared outside. It was so cold out there. His footprints had already been covered by the newly falling snow. It was a terrible night for Christmas. A horrible night to lose an angel and—

A deadly night for a human to be out.

He stepped out into the snow.

Help. Goosebumps rose on Ben's flesh, but they weren't from the cold. "Simone?" He could have sworn that he'd just heard her voice, whispering in his ear.

His breath seemed to ice before him. It was colder than hell out there.

Help.

Ben found himself walking forward. Then running. His feet seemed to fly over the thick snow.

He hadn't hurt Miles in that alley, but Miles hadn't been the only one there that night.

I forgot the kid.

Ben ran as fast as he could. He left the cabin behind, left the door open, and moments later, he found himself on a snow-covered road. Twisting trees lined both sides of that old path.

A familiar path. Simone had been here with him. She'd looked down the snow-filled road and pointed. *This way will take you out of Desolate.*

He'd known desolation for ten years. She was the only hope he had. Ben took that path because he was ready for the desolation to end.

He'd only gone a few feet when he heard... *"Help..."* A weak cry.

Ben lunged forward.

The desperate cry was greeted with grating laughter. "There's no help for you, human. You're too weak to turn, but plenty good enough to kill."

Ben rushed across the snow and saw the boy—Cale. He was on the ground, and a hunched figure was above him. The hunched figure appeared to be a male with blond hair. The male turned a bit, and Ben caught sight of his gleaming fangs.

Fuck, it's the future I saw. The vamp is going to kill the boy!

Ben's jaw locked. *Not on my watch.* Ben raced forward, grabbed the blond, and tossed the vamp into the air.

The boy screamed, *"You!"* when he saw Ben, and then the kid tried to back away, moving crab-like on the snow.

"Yes, me. It's your lucky night, kid." Ben took up a protective position in front of the human. "Because I'm your guardian angel."

Help.

The blond vamp rose. He dusted snow off his shoulders. Took his time. After a few, tense moments, his head tilted back. His eyes—a gleaming gold—met Ben's.

I know him.

The blond vampire grinned and asked, "How do you like the darkness?"

Ben's teeth were fully extended in his mouth. "You took away my life!" *This* was the bastard who'd attacked him in New York.

The vampire's face twisted with fury. "You ungrateful bastard, I *gave* you life! I sensed your potential, and I gifted you with my blood. I made you—"

"*Into a killer.*" Ben could see it now. His own reflection, in the eyes of that vampire.

The blond waved his hand carelessly. "If you want to dine on the boy, go ahead. I'm sure I'll find more prey in this Podunk town."

The kid was crying behind Ben.

"No," Ben said softly. "You won't." He advanced toward the other vampire.

The blond shook his head. "You think you're going to fight me?" His teeth snapped together with a click. "I'm over three hundred years old, I'm—"

Ben drove his fist into the vampire's jaw. That shut up the jerk. "I don't attack innocents, and you...you're as far from innocent as anyone can get. So I'm ready to give you a serious ass-kicking."

The punch had sent the vamp spinning away from Ben. The blond leaned near a tree. "As if you're innocent," the other vampire called out. "Your hands are as blood-stained as my own." The vamp whirled around. Ben saw that the vamp clutched an old, gray tree limb. The guy must've ripped it off the tree.

The vampire smiled at Ben. "Let's see how you fare in this battle, shall we?" The hint of what could've been an English accent sharpened his words as the vamp lunged for Ben with the broken tree limb.

But Ben twisted out of his way. He grabbed the vamp's wrist. Snapped it and shoved that broken limb right back at the bastard.

Back toward his heart.

"No!" The blond vampire thrust Ben away. Ben slipped in the snow, but he was able to stay upright.

The vampire screamed at Ben, "I *created* you! You don't kill me! You don't—"

Ben ran straight for him. He went in low, football-style, and grabbed the vamp's waist. Ben's momentum sent the vampire stumbling back, back—

And right into the twisting branches of the tree that waited behind the blond vamp. The branches drove into the blond's back, and then they burst through his chest.

That got your heart, you sonofabitch.

Ben left the vampire hanging on the tree. The blond's blood dripped down his chest. "Hey, bastard..." Ben growled. "*Welcome to the darkness.*"

A whimper sounded from just a few feet away. Hell. Ben turned, slowly, and found the kid staring at him with wide, desperate eyes.

Ben lifted his hands. "I'm not going to hurt you."

The boy trembled.

"I know I look like the bad guy." Okay, he *was* bad but... "I'm here to help you."

"Th-that's what the pretty lady said..."

Ben's hands fell. "What lady?"

"Th-the blonde lady, with w-wings." He shuddered. "When he bit me, I saw her. She was— was beside him. She said someone would come to help me." His gaze trekked to the vamp who was still impaled on the tree. "Is h-he...dead?"

"Mostly. He'll be gone for good when I cut off his head." *Was the boy another one of Simone's charges?* She'd guarded Ben, Jamison, and now this lost human.

The kid gulped.

"Do you still see the blonde woman?" Ben asked, barely breathing.

"No."

Dammit. But she *had* been there. Hope rose within him. If she'd been there before, Simone could appear again.

The boy whispered, "What happens now?"

"The vamp loses his head."

The kid blanched.

I have to stop scaring the boy. "What's your name?" Ben demanded. Simone had called him Cale, but that was—

"C-Cale. Cale Parker."

Ben smiled at him and hoped too much fang wasn't showing. "Cale, it's time for you to get a new life."

Because Cale wouldn't be dying alone on that snow-filled road. Not that night. Not any fucking night.

**

He'd done it.

Simone turned away from the scene on that snow-covered lane. Her wings lifted her up and carried her away from Ben and Cale. Ben had changed. In the course of one night, he'd proven that he was worthy of redemption. That he was more than just a monster.

She flew back to the little town of Desolate. Headed into the town's only bar. William and Jamison were already inside, waiting for her.

William glanced up at her approach. His lips quirked. "A demon, a shifter, and an angel walk into a bar..."

"And all hell breaks loose," Jamison finished with a laugh.

She shook her head. "I'm not an angel. Not anymore." Her wings were so light now. Because they were barely there at all. In a few more minutes, they would just be a memory.

The laughter faded from Jamison's eyes. He seemed to tense as he glanced around the bar. He swallowed, and his Adam's apple clicked. "The vamp...Ben didn't turn feral on us, did he?"

"No." It was her turn to smile. "He saved the boy, and now Ben's going to be all right." Ben would have his life back. It wouldn't just be about darkness for him. Not anymore.

He'd be happy, and that happiness was worth every sacrifice she'd made.

"What's it like?" William wanted to know. His tattoos swirled.

Simone lifted her brows.

"To love someone that much. That you'd give up everything."

She looked down at the old, scarred table top.

"Will you miss your wings?" Jamison asked when the silence stretched too long.

Simone glanced at him. "Some days, I'm sure I will." Her gaze slid to William. "And loving Ben has been the best part of my life." Her *after*-life as an angel and her human life. "He made me happy. He made me hope for things that could be."

William's eyes hardened. "But *you've* lost everything now. You'll be a vampire."

And, once again, Simone could have sworn that Jamison tensed. She frowned at him. "Why are you so nervous?"

His gaze cut around the bar. "You're not thinking of eating the bartender, are you?"

Simone laughed, and the sound surprised her. She couldn't remember the last time she'd laughed. "No, I'm good, but thanks for asking."

His shoulders sagged. "It's all changing..."

She stepped back from their table. There were only a few minutes left until midnight. "Ben proved he could be different." Simone glanced up at the bar's ceiling, but she saw so far beyond it. "So that means we stick to our deal."

Because she'd had to fight for this night. This bit of magic.

Her wings had been traded for a chance at Ben's redemption. If he proved that the man he'd been still lived inside the monster, then she could be with him.

But not as an angel.

Simone hoped that Ben liked her just as much without her wings.

She turned away from William and Jamison.

"What if..." Jamison's gravel-rough words stopped her.

Simone glanced over her shoulder.

"What if *you* go dark?"

There was worry in his eyes. The shifter cared. There was so much more to him than just a growling beast. "I won't."

He shook his head. "You don't know what I've seen."

Simone inclined her head toward him. "Of course, I do. It was my magic, after all. From the beginning, I knew what could happen to Ben...and to me. Why do you think I fought so hard for him?"

Because she'd either survive with him.

Or fall with her vamp.

***

Jamison watched Simone walk away. When the door closed behind her, he reached for the whiskey bottle. His hands were shaking.

"Sonofabitch," he muttered, stunned. "She knew all along that she'd be losing her head."

"No." William's gaze was on the door. A faint grin tilted his lips. "Simone knew that she *could*. She just loved her vamp so much it didn't matter." His fingers drummed on the table. "Fucking insanity." He grabbed his glass. He was drinking spiked eggnog. He tapped the eggnog against Jamison's whiskey bottle. "You know what they say...angels are the craziest ones in the bunch."

"Uh..." Jamison hadn't known that anyone said that.

"They're also the ones who fall the hardest." William drained his glass. "That vamp had better be worth her fall, or else he'll be getting another visit from us next year."

Jamison nodded. "Damn straight."

"And this time..." The tattoos darkened around William's neck. "The ghost from his past will kick his *ass*."

Jamison chugged his whiskey. William hadn't seen Ben when the stake entered Simone's heart, so the demon didn't know...

The vampire loves her. Without her, Ben was broken. Jamison had watched Ben shatter.

No, there wouldn't be any ass kicking necessary. But maybe they'd still pay a visit to the vampire and his ex-angel, just for old time's sake.

And to make sure Simone's future never involves her being thrown away like garbage in an unmarked grave.

That image wouldn't be leaving his mind any time soon.

Jamison motioned to the bartender.

But I'll do my freaking best to drink that sight away.

CHAPTER TEN

"We're staying here?" Cale asked him, squinting at Ben's cabin. His face looked less than pleased. "It's not about to cave in, is it?"

"Kid, you lived in an alley. Don't knock my home."

Cale flushed.

Aw, hell. Ben was so not good at the whole using-tact-with-humans bit. He'd have to work on that.

He'd talked with Cale, used some compulsion, and discovered that the boy was completely alone in the world. Both of Cale's parents were dead. There were no other family members. The boy didn't have anyone.

Or at least, he hadn't.

"Go on inside," Ben directed gruffly. The front door was still open. When he'd raced out earlier, securing the place had been his last thought. "I'll light a fire and get you warmed up."

Cale took a step forward, but then stopped. "Promise not to bite me?"

He'd already promised *seven* times. Ben glared at the guy. "Don't tempt me."

Cale offered a weak grin. "Sorry. Still getting used to the whole vampires-are-real thing."

"Yeah, it takes some time." Wait until the kid found out about the demons...

Cale slid into the cabin. "I wish the angel would come back," he threw over his shoulder.

Me, too. Ben rubbed his chest. His heart just ached.

"I liked her," Cale added. "She was—*damn, nice tree!*"

That sad, sagging tree was nice? Ben stomped in behind the kid, then he froze in his tracks. The tree was still sagging, but now it was also covered in dozens of ornaments and sparkling lights, and the thing just glowed.

A warm fire crackled in the nearby fireplace.

"Guess someone has the Christmas spirit, huh, vamp?" Cale was grinning as he stared at the tree, and, on his face, in his wide eyes, Ben saw...hope.

The same hope was rising in his chest. The tree shouldn't look like that. And the place—it *shouldn't* smell of vanilla. But it did.

"Be here," Ben whispered, begged.

Then the little clock on his table clicked. The sound was so soft, but he heard it, and his gaze slid to the clock's face.

Midnight.

Christmas. This was the day that Simone lost her wings.

He shook his head. He didn't want that. She had to stay safe. She had to stay—

A floorboard creaked behind him. Ben whirled and saw her in the doorway. Flecks of snow were in her hair. And her eyes...they were golden now.

The gold of a vampire.

But when he looked at her, Ben just saw his angel.

"Merry Christmas," Simone whispered.

Ben could only stare at her.

"Hey!" Cale's voice cracked with excitement. "It's my angel!"

Simone shook her head. Sadness slid into her eyes. "Not anymore..."

Ben ran toward her. He wrapped his arms around her and held her as tightly as he could. She was real against him. Warm. Not a dream. Not a memory.

"Always," he said as he squeezed her, and he knew the squeeze was probably way too hard. "You'll always be my angel." Ben kissed her. Deep and hard, wild and desperate. With passion. With love. With everything that he had.

Because to Ben, Simone *was* everything. Every hope. Every dream. The reason he had to fight the darkness.

She tasted like heaven. Her arms wrapped around him. She met his kiss with the same wild hunger that consumed Ben.

His hands trailed over her back. He caressed her delicate muscles and—

Ben lifted his head. "Your wings?"

Her golden gaze held his. "It was a fair trade."

He wasn't so sure. "I'm not worth them."

"To me..." Her fingers slid over his jaw. "You're worth everything."

The cold air blew in behind her. The snow was falling again.

"Um, are you two...like a thing?" Cale asked nervously.

Ben dropped to his knees before Simone. This was so long overdue. He pulled the ring box from his pocket. "I kept this...it was all I had of you." He opened the box. The ring gleamed. A ring he'd had made just for her.

The woman who'd stolen his heart and held it tightly for ten years.

He lifted the box toward her. "Will you marry me?"

Simone smiled at him. A smile that lit her whole face and had made Ben's heart race in his chest. "Yes," she said, laughing. "Always—*yes!*" Then she tackled him.

Ben fell back onto the hard floor, and he found himself laughing as she held him. The cold didn't matter. The darkness he'd known—it was gone. There was only light.

Love.

Hope.

There was only Simone.

He hugged her, keeping Simone close to his heart, and Ben knew that he'd just been given the best gift of all. A second chance, with the one woman who made his vampire life worth living.

THE END

A NOTE FROM THE AUTHOR

Thank you so much for reading A VAMPIRE'S CHRISTMAS CAROL. I appreciate you taking the time to read Ben's story!

Ever since I was a child, I've loved the Charles Dickens classic tale. And, each time that I read the story, Tiny Tim makes me tear up even as the character reminds me that we can always find wonder in the holiday season.

I certainly hope that your holiday season is filled with wonder.

If you'd like to stay updated on my releases and sales, please join my newsletter list.

https://cynthiaeden.com/newsletter/

Again, thank you for reading A VAMPIRE'S CHRISTMAS CAROL.

Best,
Cynthia Eden
cynthiaeden.com

ABOUT THE AUTHOR

Cynthia Eden is a *New York Times*, *USA Today*, *Digital Book World*, and *IndieReader* best-seller.

Cynthia writes sexy tales of contemporary romance, romantic suspense, and paranormal romance. Since she began writing full-time in 2005, Cynthia has written over one hundred novels and novellas.

Cynthia lives along the Alabama Gulf Coast. She loves romance novels, horror movies, and chocolate.

For More Information

- *cynthiaeden.com*
- *facebook.com/cynthiaedenfanpage*

HER OTHER WORKS

Wilde Ways

- Protecting Piper (Book 1)
- Guarding Gwen (Book 2)
- Before Ben (Book 3)
- The Heart You Break (Book 4)
- Fighting For Her (Book 5)
- Ghost Of A Chance (Book 6)
- Crossing The Line (Book 7)
- Counting On Cole (Book 8)
- Chase After Me (Book 9)
- Say I Do (Book 10)

Dark Sins

- Don't Trust A Killer (Book 1)
- Don't Love A Liar (Book 2)

Lazarus Rising

- Never Let Go (Book One)
- Keep Me Close (Book Two)
- Stay With Me (Book Three)
- Run To Me (Book Four)
- Lie Close To Me (Book Five)
- Hold On Tight (Book Six)
- Lazarus Rising Volume One (Books 1 to 3)

- Lazarus Rising Volume Two (Books 4 to 6)

Dark Obsession Series

- Watch Me (Book 1)
- Want Me (Book 2)
- Need Me (Book 3)
- Beware Of Me (Book 4)
- Only For Me (Books 1 to 4)

Mine Series

- Mine To Take (Book 1)
- Mine To Keep (Book 2)
- Mine To Hold (Book 3)
- Mine To Crave (Book 4)
- Mine To Have (Book 5)
- Mine To Protect (Book 6)
- Mine Box Set Volume 1 (Books 1-3)
- Mine Box Set Volume 2 (Books 4-6)

Bad Things

- The Devil In Disguise (Book 1)
- On The Prowl (Book 2)
- Undead Or Alive (Book 3)
- Broken Angel (Book 4)
- Heart Of Stone (Book 5)
- Tempted By Fate (Book 6)
- Wicked And Wild (Book 7)
- Saint Or Sinner (Book 8)
- Bad Things Volume One (Books 1 to 3)
- Bad Things Volume Two (Books 4 to 6)
- Bad Things Deluxe Box Set (Books 1 to 6)

Bite Series

- Forbidden Bite (Bite Book 1)
- Mating Bite (Bite Book 2)

Blood and Moonlight Series

- Bite The Dust (Book 1)
- Better Off Undead (Book 2)
- Bitter Blood (Book 3)
- Blood and Moonlight (The Complete Series)

Purgatory Series

- The Wolf Within (Book 1)
- Marked By The Vampire (Book 2)
- Charming The Beast (Book 3)
- Deal with the Devil (Book 4)
- The Beasts Inside (Books 1 to 4)

Bound Series

- Bound By Blood (Book 1)
- Bound In Darkness (Book 2)
- Bound In Sin (Book 3)
- Bound By The Night (Book 4)
- Bound in Death (Book 5)
- Forever Bound (Books 1 to 4)

Other Romantic Suspense

- Never Gonna Happen
- One Hot Holiday
- Secret Admirer
- First Taste of Darkness
- Sinful Secrets
- Until Death
- Christmas With A Spy

Made in United States
North Haven, CT
05 December 2022

28015636R00065